SEEING THINGS

By the same author:

(for children)

THE BLINDFOLD TRACK

SECRETS

DEAR COMRADE

A KNOT OF SPELLS

ZAK

SEEING THINGS

Frances Thomas

LONDON
VICTOR GOLLANCZ LTD
1986

First published in Great Britain 1986
by Victor Gollancz Ltd,
14 Henrietta Street, London WC2E 8QJ

© Frances Thomas 1986

British Library Cataloguing in Publication Data
Thomas, Frances
  Seeing things.
  I. Title
  823'.914[F]   PR6070.H6/

ISBN 0-575-03757-1

Typeset at The Spartan Press Ltd, Lymington, Hants
and printed in Great Britain by St Edmundsbury Press
Bury St Edmunds, Suffolk

For Richard

'Who can go further? Shall I seek visions? Many have tried them and found only illusions.'

St Augustine

SEEING THINGS

Chapter 1

"Difference?" said Father Mack, getting excited, "My dear girl, there's all the difference in the world. *Con-* and you have a purely commemorative act, a mere symbol. *Trans-* and there is the real thing, the true mystical transformation of the Bloody and Bod . . ."

Everyone stopped eating, except deaf Lady Bathmaker, who continued to stab carrots with her fork. Father Mack was dismayed at himself. "I — er – I . . ."

"When I was a gel," said Lady Bathmaker, tuning in to an earlier stage in the conversation, "I decided that it was quite impossible to believe in God, and do you know, I've never for one moment gone back on that."

"What I meant to say . . ." went on Father Mack.

"Of course," said Antonia gently. But she launched into the attack again almost immediately. "I still can't understand, Father, why you have to believe in *cannibalism*. What's wrong with a symbol, after all?"

The priest flinched, and his wine-red face topped by its heavy cliff of black hair seemed to grow a shade darker. He was not, Hugo observed, enjoying the process of being quizzed by a woman. After all, the Catholic Church recognised only two types of womanhood, Eve and the Virgin Mary. Eve was the one who asked all the questions. "No one," said Father Mack, a little thickly, "has ever accused me of cannibalism before."

"Of course," went on Lady Bathmaker, who wore a grey wig at a rakish angle and the ruins of a quite extraordinary beauty, "most of one's friends *did* believe in God. There was no question about it then. One believed."

Hugo sat in some discomfort, feeling that his carefully planned dinner party was now in ruins. How on earth had he let a discussion on transubstantiation get in the way of the *boeuf en croûte*?

"I mean," pursued Antonia relentlessly, "why is it necessary for a *spiritual* experience to depend on the consumption of actual flesh and blood?" She paused, a piece of perfectly *saignant* beef half-way to her mouth.

"Flesh, flesh, how art thou fishified!" said Lady Bathmaker unexpectedly. Father Mack was momentarily unable to continue.

"Lady Bathmaker," said Hugo, "a few more green beans? A slice of beef?"

"Talking of fish," continued Lady Bathmaker, "did you know that Madame de Pompadour's real name was Antoinette Poisson?" She smiled squarely at Father Mack, showing discoloured teeth.

Father Mack regained his impetus. "How," he went on, "can fallible human clay respond, if not through the physical? We are not, my dear young lady, beings of air and purity, like the angels. We are creatures of dirt and corruption. Yet through our vile senses we perceive all that is good and holy, and so Christ has chosen to enter our bodies with a penetration that is similar to . . ."

"Some more *pommes Anna*, Father?" said Hugo hurriedly. He remembered of old how steamy Father Mack could be once he got launched on the subject of the Mystical Bridegroom.

"Madame de Fish!" said Lady Bathmaker with a surprisingly deep chortle. "It always makes me laugh!"

"That's another thing," added Antonia. "This business of the Immaculate Conception. Honestly, I do find it offensive."

Father Mack fixed her with a shark-like smile. "Oh really, my dear. Why is that?"

"Because, Father, I don't find anything to be ashamed of in the working of my body, and goodness, if the Mother of God . . ."

"Sex again!" said Father Mack. "You know it sometimes seems to me that non-Catholics are obsessed with sex!"

"I had an RC friend once," said Lady Bathmaker, continuing on her joyfully oblivious monologue. "She used to say that she took as a model in life the Holy Virgin. My dear! When I met her a few years later, she was neither holy nor a virgin, I can assure you."

"Shall I collect your plates?" asked Hugo, noting how Antonia had left a large chunk of expensive fillet congealing on hers. "I'm afraid there's only a little Grand Marnier soufflé to follow. I meant to make a syllabub yesterday but somehow I didn't find the time."

"Poor darling, he's so busy!" said Antonia.

"Well, not exactly," said Hugo, "but I had to see my publisher and there were some books to go back to the London Library and in the evening . . ."

"I tell people," said Lady Bathmaker, "that I live next to a famous writer. Everyone's most impressed. My dear! The self-discipline! To sit at a typewriter all day!"

Father Mack relinquished his hold on the Immaculate Conception. "I think we can claim a little bit of the glory for that, eh, Hugo? I think we can bask in reflected pride. I remember once how I made you write out a Latin prose four times and . . ."

"I'm afraid you'll have to excuse me for a moment," said Hugo. "I have to go and beat up egg whites."

". . . and of course you were fed up with me, but I said, and I remember saying it, one day, Hugo, you'll appreciate that only perfection will do. I bet you don't remember me saying that, do you, eh, my lad?"

"You were a hard taskmaster," said Hugo.

"And my goodness, hasn't it paid off? Eh? What is it, four novels to date?"

"Three," said Hugo. "Now if you'll all . . ."

"And what's in the pipeline now, Hugo, may we enquire?"

But this was worse than God. "Well, I . . ."

"Oh, Hugo's writing a book on visions," said Antonia, who had forgiven Father Mack even if he had not forgiven her.

"*Fishing?*" exclaimed Lady Bathmaker.

"No, Lady Bathmaker. *Visions*. *Hugo* is *writing* a *book* on visions."

"Goodness, my girl, you don't have to shout. Visions, now, Mr Swann. Would that be Roman Catholic visions?"

It might have been, except that the book was going rather badly at the moment. But Antonia, who had previously been very scathing about the subject, rose up with enthusiasm. "Oh yes, he believes in them all you know, and he's got this fascinating theory that . . ."

"Well, perhaps not exactly *all*," said Hugo. In fact he had tried to argue one evening the truth of visionary experience simply to counterbalance what seemed to him to be Antonia's unthinking and obdurate scepticism. Now the ghosts of those ill-considered words rose up to haunt him. The visionaries he wanted to write about were not what he privately considered the 'Hollywood' ones, those commercialised and vulgar incidents involving ignorant peasant children, but the more refined and private experiences of the great mystics. The rest were simply another of the embarrassments which all intelligent Catholics had to swallow.

"But I do feel that in certain cases, Saint Teresa for example, the visionary attains to a level of perception that . . . look, I really must see to those eggs. I won't be a moment."

"There!" he said as he put the soufflé on the table.

"Oh, well done!"

"Isn't that perfect?"

"Clever boy!" said Antonia. "You know, I can never get mine to rise, as the bishop said to the . . . whoops, sorry, Father!"

Father Mack's smile might have been cast in ice. "You don't need to apologise to me, my dear. Just because I wear my collar a different way round doesn't mean that I'm innocent of the world and its ways."

"My tongue simply runs away with me, I'm afraid."

"But *so* charmingly," said Father Mack with insincerity. "Hugo, you were about to say something on the subject of Saint Teresa."

"Was I? Oh yes, it was simply that . . . Lady Bathmaker, please don't wait. There's cream if you like."

"Tell me," said Lady Bathmaker, sniffing her plate with elegant greed, "do you fold in the whites with a metal spoon? They say you should, don't they, but I never do. But then you see my soufflés are always flat as doormats."

"I use a copper bowl. And a pinch of cream of tartar."

"Saint Teresa," repeated Father Mack.

"I don't really think anyone wants to hear my feelings about Saint Teresa."

"Darling, I'm fascinated!" Did Antonia wink at him across the table?

"No, I'm sure."

"Do go on."

"Well, it's hardly anything so grand as a theory. But it's just that we're so cynical today about religion. . . ."

"*You* might be cynical about religion," admonished Father Mack, "*I* am not. Do continue."

"Some people are so cynical about religion that they deny it any reality at all. We — they — assume everything religious is a second-rate substitute for sex."

"Well, isn't it?" asked Antonia. This time the wink was unmistakable.

Hugo felt himself floundering. "For example, take Saint Teresa's famous vision."

"What famous vision, my darling?"

"You must know the statue by Bernini, where the angel is plunging a fiery sword into her breast. . . ."

"A fiery sword," said Antonia, "just fancy that!"

"There you are! You just can't accept for a moment, can you, that it's anything but a rather bad Freudian joke?"

"A fiery sword," Antonia repeated. "Well, well."

"Whereas what you won't let yourself see," said Hugo, wishing he had never let himself in for this, "is that the visionary might really experience a unity with the divine that the rest of us can never reach."

"Exactly!" said Father Mack.

"Exactly," murmured Antonia.

"You can mock," said Hugo. "But did you know that when they opened Saint Teresa's body after her death, they found that there really was a wound in her heart? A wound with charred edges, as though something hot and sharp had been plunged into it."

"There!" said Father Mack. "Now explain that if you can with all your clever psychological theories!"

"I had a friend once," said Lady Bathmaker, "who saw snakes everywhere. My dears! Her bed was alive with them, they writhed all over her floor, they hung from the trees!"

"And what happened to her, Lady Bathmaker?" asked Antonia politely.

"Well, you see, they'd married her at seventeen to a frightful fellow. Of course she was a virgin, in those days everyone was, and quite, quite ignorant. Her husband, it seemed, was not only impotent, he was quite uninterested too. And poor girl, she being so ignorant, didn't even know what it was she wasn't having. Hence the snakes, d'you see?"

"I'm not sure I . . ." said Father Mack dangerously.

"But then one day the husband's best friend found out all about this. Now he was a charming man, though something of a philanderer, and he took it upon himself to fill in the missing parts of her education."

"And did it work?" said Antonia.

"My dear! I only saw her once afterwards but she looked radiantly happy. And of course no more snakes. The only problem was that she kept having children. The husband must have known at this point that something was up, since I'm sure *he* didn't believe in immaculate conception, but as far as one knows he was perfectly happy to be allowed to get on with his stamp collection. Now the eldest boy has inherited the title, and he has no idea there isn't a drop of noble blood in his veins. It would cause the most fearful ructions in Debrett, I imagine." She paused and looked around her, her eyes glittering redly. "So you see, in spite of what you say, I put most of the problems in the world down to bad sex. That's why it's so important. I think everyone should have as much sex as they can." She sighed and wiped a bead of moisture from the corner of her eye. "While they're young, that is."

It was not surprising after such an evening that Hugo should find it difficult to sleep. What a fiasco! Antonia so teasing, Lady Bathmaker so deaf and Father Mack so — well, so Father Mackish. Lady Bathmaker's parting comment was the last straw. As everyone was standing to take their farewells, she went over to his desk (his desk! his private domain!) and studied the contents with interest. Propped up against the Thesaurus was a large black and white photograph of Donatello's David peering out coyly underneath the rim of his enchanting hat. "Ah, Mr Swann," she said loudly, "I'm so glad you like having beautiful young men to look at!" Antonia snorted and Father Mack shot him a very strange look across the room.

But the thing was, he did enjoy looking at David. Was it with an erotic tingle? Oh dear. Should he not perhaps be a little more guarded about private pleasures? To most people even the very state of catholicism meant you were something less than a man. Did David's picture stamp him with the taint of eunuchry?

Yet David was beautiful, and what was wrong with beauty? Beauty! Such a thin, pallid term in today's critical coinage. A whole new brutal generation of words like commitment and relevance and validity had risen up to take its place, shoving aside its intangible delights. Did Donatello's shepherd boy show Hugo, who liked having him there, to be a closet queer? Would Primavera — another love — be any less dubious? Was Hugo odd? Was he committed? Was he indeed relevant?

Oh those fair frail medieval faces! They looked in fact very much like his own, which may have been the reason why he favoured them. But also they sang to him of a world clothed in mysterious grandeur, a cathedral world of fierce extremes, of glowing colour and deep shadow; a world which God, jealous and demanding as He was, held securely in His arms. How had such a world shrunk into the cold, pragmatic and vicious place He inhabited now? Why had God unloosed His grip?

Or perhaps it was only upon himself that God's hold had been loosed. He could still recall, as though it were an elusive and lovely dream, the incandescent year of his conversion, a year in which Father Mack had played the role of mentor. There had been a moment when emerging from the muddy sea of adolescence he had found himself blinking, looking around, waiting for something to happen.

Then God had called him.

He remembered it with clarity. There he was in the refectory struggling with a pork chop when the Voice sounded quite clearly inside his head: 'I want you.' It did not matter that for ever afterwards in his memory this moment was linked with the smell of cabbage and boiled potatoes, the dead sheen of varnished wood and the raucous din of two hundred boys.

Of course he had not responded straight away. In fact, immediately afterwards he looked sheepishly around him to make sure he had not done anything foolish which others might have noticed and then returned to his plate. The next day, on his way to the baths, carrying a damp towel, there it was again. 'I want you.' By now he knew who it was, who was calling him and went straight away to the chapel, where he knelt before the altar with its veiled tabernacle, its gilded rail, its red cushions and its carvings of writhing wood.

Everything seemed to fall into place at once after that, and he took to fervour with a single-mindedness that amused his friends and even embarrassed some of the Brothers. Not Father Mack though. Father Mack and Hugo sat up night after night, discussing angels and original sin, purgatory and penance, with an enthusiasm which most of his contemporaries reserved for female anatomy.

Of course, it had not continued like that forever. Hugo had left school, and gone to Oxford where he had slept with a girl or two, taken a cold draught of Marxism and an intoxicating gulp of

Freud. Faith was never again to be the thing it once was. Soon after he left Oxford, he wrote his first novel. This, described by one reviewer as a 'charming fantasy' (and by another as 'whimsical artifice'), retold the story of Pygmalion and Galatea, in *fin de siècle* France. Galatea, bored and indignant at being summoned to life to be the fantasy girl of an elderly sculptor whom she would not have chosen for herself, sets off in search of her own adventures, but is so disgusted by the young men she meets in Paris, that she rents a studio for herself and there sculpts her own dream love, an exquisite young man. The story ended just as the statue she had made was starting to come to life. The novel had been a great success and was still doing well in paperback. Then had followed a more serious work, describing a young man's Catholic upbringing; this was received with somewhat chillier enthusiasm. His last, an even more ambitious attempt to anatomise a fading marriage, had not done at all well. Perhaps he had stepped out of his depth in thinking he could describe marriage, a state of which he as yet knew nothing. Or perhaps a kind of lethargy of spirit had set in.

At any rate, he found the lethargy had infected his faith too. Of course he still practised, but the rapture was no longer there, and he missed it. Faith had become another habit, like going to the dentist; what would he do, for the rest of his life, if rapture had gone?

Chapter 2

The end of a Saturday afternoon, raw and dank, September mimicking November, the air gone sour and stale with a yellow stain like nicotine spreading slowly across the sky. Doors had been shut and lamps lit behind curtains. Perhaps those with a warm fire and a family at home might find comfort in the contrast with the bleak afternoon, but for Father Bob Joyce walking alone through dingy South London streets there would be only the cold ritual of confession and an empty flat to follow. At the end of Thornton Street crouched Saint Gertrude's, squat and angry, Victorian brickwork livid beneath the eerie sky, dwarfing the diminishing perspectives of the terrace which led to it.

Father Joyce reached the church and opened the heavy door. In the dim vestibule piles of hymn books mouldered and racks of pious pamphlets grew limp and dog-eared. His footsteps echoed emptily on the floor of flagstones and metal heating grilles. This evening the church was a cavern of purplish shadows lit only faintly by the metallic drizzle that came through plain glass windows. An edge of light defined the white altar table with its simple cross and large candles, and disappeared into the depths where Tabernacle and Chalice waited, the intangible brooding Presence. Though Father Joyce had cleared away much devotional clutter when he had arrived in the parish five years previously, Saint Anthony and the Virgin still stood on their plinths, black beady eyes staring into the emptiness.

But it was not empty. Today there was someone in the church, kneeling in the front pew, a strange woman hunched in a moth-eaten fur. Gypsy earrings flashed as she turned her head towards him with a wild expression in her eyes. She jumped to her feet and stared at him with a beaky face full of shadows. She looked ill.

"Oh," said the priest in surprise. "Can I . . ."

"No," she said abruptly, "you most decidedly cannot."

"Is there a problem?"

"There's a problem all right. A problem is what there is."

"Do let's talk about it."

"Talk?" she said scornfully. "Talk? What the hell would talking do?"

"It can help. It often helps. Let's give it a try. We can go up to my flat if you'd like."

"No." she said, "I do not like. I don't know why I came here anyway. I must be mad. What could you possibly do, you silly man in a dress? How could you help?"

The right words must be there; it was simply a matter of finding them. "A trouble shared, you know. I really would like to help you."

"Balls," she said, "you really wouldn't, I'm telling you. If there's one thing that would really make you want to throw up, it would be listening to me. No, I'm off. It was a great mistake coming here in the first place."

"If you . . ." But too late. With a whiff of mothballs she pushed past him and ran out down the aisle. Her high heels click-click-clicked and then died away into silence.

The great wooden door slammed behind her, resounded. Father Joyce stood there for some time, watching the space where she had been standing. A mad woman, a crazy woman, but a woman who had wanted to talk or she would not have come here.

And what had he done for her? She had looked at him in contempt and run away. A silly man in a dress. The cloth was supposed to symbolise his sacrifice of himself for humanity's sake; but as usual it turned out to be only a barrier.

Beyond the sacristy door the yard was in darkness with a dank smell; was it the drains again? Once there had been a priest's house here, an extravagant fantasy of red brick and Gothic crenellations which had housed two priests and a curate. Now the presbytery was gone, sold at some profit to a developer who had managed to cram in a block of eight flats on the site. The curate had been dispensed with and Father Joyce managed the parish on his own with the help of Sister Mahony, a nun who lived in a hostel some way away, and a few assiduous parish workers like Mr Painscastle who knew everybody's business. Father Joyce lived in what had once been the housekeeper's flat, three rooms over the church hall reached by an iron staircase. He wanted his flat to be a place where the lonely, the displaced or the worried might feel free to sit round his fire and chat over cocoa, but nobody came. He tried to brighten up the walls with orange paint and pictures of rural scenes but it made no difference. The previous year he had been forced to close down the youth club after its membership had dwindled to a group of skinheads, not even Catholics, who called out racial abuse and smashed up the record player.

The flat was cold tonight; he was economising. And he had forgotten to switch on the heating in the church; the mad woman had driven it from his mind. Just time to make himself a cup of tea, though. A slug of whisky would have helped no end to drive away the dreary chill of confession but you could not absolve in a cloud of booze.

We are all, he said to himself, as he sipped his tea and gazed through his square of window to the dreary roofscape beyond, we are all God's creatures, even the mad and the boring.

Yet if he was prepared to go to them, why were they not willing to come to him?

There is a strange light peculiar to convents, a cool washed seaside brightness, though perhaps it is only the same light as everywhere else, filtered through curtains of thick cream lace, or bounced off glittering parquet or held cupped in milky marble. Convents are perhaps no different from any other institution and the clear thin voices of singing nuns are simply the voices of any women raised in harmony. Especially now that the heavy black habits have mostly been swept away and nuns have redefined their vocations in more practical ways, a convent should be merely another place where people live and work.

The Convent of the Seven Sorrows stood, grey and Gothic, high on a suburban hill from which you might have seen far off in the distance the domes and towers of the City, shining like a glimpse of paradise. But the convent, girded in dense woods, spreading lavishly over acres of some of the most potentially valuable real estate in the suburbs, did not care for the proximity. It was God's world and not man's that counted here. When you passed through the great iron gates into the padded silence you left the frivolous and the temporal behind you. Even for the two hundred-odd schoolgirls, it was like a time warp when they passed through those gates. It was a kingdom within a kingdom, a place secure unto itself, a fastness of peace.

It had stood there, on its high hill, for less than a hundred years, though so solid and extensive was it that it seemed to have been there for far longer. Many years before, when the area was all wild woodland, one of the Georges (the second, was it, or perhaps the third — the nuns were vague about human history) had built a hunting lodge which still stood, now housing a junior school. You could walk around the muddy grounds for an hour or so and not cover the same yard twice. The convent itself was rambling and extravagant, six great storeys with a huge central staircase winding round and round into distant heights. Some of the more imaginative girls — though there were not too many of these at the Seven Sorrows — used to speculate about ghost nuns inhabiting lost locked rooms, corridors where no living foot had trodden for years, or corners where strange rites took place at midnight, far from chapel and cloakroom and the familiar school highways.

But even at the Seven Sorrows things were changing. The heavy serge habit had been gone for some years and nuns could be seen to possess hair and legs, just like everybody else. A nun helped the priest distribute communion, touching the Sacred Host in a way that would have been thought sacrilegious in the past. Nuns went home and had holidays with their families, they jumped on trains and had cheque books. They knew about *Dallas* and the *Daily Mirror*, they could take baths, like everybody else, with all their clothes off. They used Tampax and went into Marks and Spencer to buy underwear. Vatican Two had come not so much as a gust of fresh air than as a raging hurricane.

And had it improved things? Well, opinions on that subject were divided. Old Sister Aloysius was very sure that it had not. Sister Mark, who left the convent every day to work with deprived children, welcomed every reform.

But nobody asked Sister Scholastica. Nobody would have done. Sister Scholastica kept her thoughts to herself.

The Angelus bell rang out, two clear notes, and Sister Scholastica thought of the Noonday Devil. No matter that he had been banished from the liturgy along with limbo, indulgences, guardian angels and Saint Christopher, he still stalked through her day, a dark shadow that disfigured her intentions and sapped her will, a creeping insidious figure of medieval aspect who thrust himself obscenely between intention and achievement. I *will* be good, she had said to herself, echoing Queen Victoria, and with at least equal determination, but where was goodness now? Where in the tangle of her thoughts was that hard crystalline purity, that refined absence of self? The demon still grinned and the routines of prayer and work which should have pulled her through the day in safe hands no longer worked.

There were two sins against the Holy Ghost and despair was one of them. Get thee behind me, Satan.

Before her, IIIa bent over a Latin exercise. They were the low stream and next year they would all drop Latin anyway. Only her icy discipline kept them fixed to their books; yet it was a thankless task. "What does *eadem* mean, Sister?" "Sister, I can't do number three," "Sister, this doesn't make sense."

Anne Marie Kelly was restless today, shifting in her seat and trying to attract Rosemary Welch's attention. A white pudding, Anne Marie, stupid Irish, the worst sort of Catholic, only there because of a bursary and the misplaced compassion of Mother John, the previous Reverend Mother. Such a girl would have been far better off at the Sacred Heart Comprehensive where she could mix with girls of her own sort. What good would Latin and great expectations do Anne Marie Kelly?

"Sister, Sister, I'm stuck on number six."

"Then leave it you silly child and go on to number seven. Or is number seven beyond you too?"

The girl looked up. Seeing Sister's porcelain face, the heavy glittering glasses, the unblinking vivid blue eyes magnified and swimming through thick lenses, she looked down again, defeated.

"Sister, I can't do *Non mos est noster hostem adiuvare.*"

Sister put her head on one side and smiled faintly. "Can you not, Alexandra Wood? What shall we do about you? A brain transplant, perhaps?"

Giggles. Then silence. Sister drummed her fingers on her desk. Outside she could see from her raised dais the garden walk where a group of sixth-formers strolled, laughing and superior, clutching files. Joanna Price, Milly Cousins . . . and talking to them both, Rachel Gold. Rachel carried a red shoulder bag, and the mass of her bronze-mahogany hair fell over her shoulders unbound against all the school rules. As she threw back her head and laughed, the sun struck sparks from her hair and her dark eyes glowed, a pre-Raphaelite angel in school uniform. In spite of herself, Sister continued to stare at Rachel as the girl crossed through the shrub border and out of sight.

And meanwhile Anne Marie Kelly, sensing the nun's distraction, propped up her books to make a shield and whispered to Rosemary Welch. "I've got something to tell you, right? A secret. I'll tell you at break. And you're not to tell anyone. Anyone."

"All right," said Carmen Carmichael. "I know you're there, somewhere. I know you're lurking somewhere and I'm going to . . . ah, here you are you old bastard, behind the ketchup. Well, I'm going to have a bloody great swig, no water or ice, see if I care, anyway it doesn't matter very much now, does it? Look, Mother Mary Patrick, look Father O'Toole, old Carmen's on the booze again, and you're not going to stop her now. Silly man in a dress! *Do let's talk about it*! No, do let's not. Do let's do anything else than talk about it. . . ."

Suddenly she broke off and sank down on to the bed. The room smelt of oil and turps, but beneath it all was another faint sweetish smell though perhaps it was only mothballs. Clothes and unfinished canvasses were strewn everywhere, bright jagged abstracts with screeching primary colours next to the landscapes she churned out for a living, sunset over autumn woods, misty horizons, woolly trees bleeding into pink skies. In the sink, plates peeped out of a bowl of grey water on the surface of which floated a ring of scarlet oil paint.

"Oh God," said Carmen softly, "Oh God, God, God, whatever am I going to do now?"

"First I saw this light," said Anne Marie, "and then I saw *her*."

"I don't believe you. You're making it up," said Rosemary Welch.

"I am *not*."

"You are."

"Are you calling me a liar?"

"Well, you must admit it's a bit . . ."

"*Are* you calling me a liar?"

"Honestly, Anne Marie . . ."

"I don't care if you don't believe me. I'm telling the truth."

"Yes, but Anne Marie . . ."

"My mum believes me. She didn't at first but she believes me now. Or she nearly does."

"Well, I . . ."

"*She* knows I'm telling the truth. I am. You'll see."

"Yes, but look . . . hey, Anne Marie, don't go! What did she look like? What did she wear? Anne Marie! Anne *Marie*!"

"Oh, I've had such a day!" laughed Sister Mark, pulling off

leather driving gauntlets and crash helmet. "I can't tell you!" Her short urchin haircut was spikily exposed, but her veil was close at hand in her bag, and she whipped it out and tied it quickly round her head. "That straight, Sister?" she asked Sister Charles Borromeo, who said she thought it was. "Young Gary managed to get hold of a knife today, goodness only knows how, and you see, they'd just sent this new social worker, a sweet girl, but no *idea*, fresh from college, and he backed into a corner and stood there *menacing*. Of course all the kids got hysterical, and poor — what was her name? — Janet, I think, poor Janet didn't know where to put herself. So I just said, come along now Gary, you don't want to be killing a nun now, do you, and he looked at me and dropped the knife. He was like a lamb after that. It was everybody being frightened, you see, that egged him on. Oh Sister, is that a kettle just boiled? I'm dying of thirst!"

"I really don't know how you do it," shuddered old Sister Aloysius. "I find it hard enough dealing with our girls here sometimes, and goodness knows they're nice enough lasses. But all this social work and gadding about on motorcycles! I'm afraid I'm too old a dog to learn new tricks."

"Well, you may have to learn them soon," said Sister Imelda from across the room. "No, sit down, Sister Mark, I'll make you a cup."

"Bless you, my darling." Sister Mark sank into a chair and thrust out her legs. "Whoops! Not too far now, Sister," she admonished herself as her skirt rode above her knees.

"I should think not indeed," said Sister Aloysius. "Sister Imelda, what do you mean?"

"Well if you haven't heard, my dear, I'm not going to be the one. Milk and sugar, Sister Mark?"

"Heard what, for heaven's sake?"

"Do you want me to take the tea bag out now, or shall I leave it to brew a bit?"

"Oh leave it, Sister, please. Strong, strong, *strong* is what I need today."

"Perhaps God has made me invisible in my old age," said Sister Aloysius testily, "but I was under the impression that I had asked a question."

"You'll hear about it soon enough I expect."

"I would prefer to hear about it *now*, since you have raised the matter."

"Yes, go on, Sister Imm. You've roused our curiosity."

"Oh, very well. I suppose there can't be any harm in it. I don't think it's meant to be a secret. Rev Muv's just had this letter from the Bishop."

"And. . . ?"

"Well, my dears." Sister Imelda, who had finely arched brows, raised them knowingly. "Here it all is. Rationalisation. The twentieth century, bless its little heart."

"I may be old," said Sister Aloysius, "and most probably I am stupid as well. But . . ."

"Comprehensive schools, Sister! No more privilege for rich little Catholic girls! Throw them into the melting pot with Sister Mark's little darlings. That's the thing now."

"Sister, you don't mean they want to make the *Seven Sorrows* into a *comprehensive school*?"

"Worse than that, I'm afraid. They're talking about closing it down altogether."

"Dear God. Dear blessed God," said Sister Aloysius faintly.

"The convent is apparently uneconomical," Sister Imelda said, giving a little laugh. "If they pull it down they could sell the land and rehouse us all. I understand there is plenty of empty space in tower blocks these days."

Sister Charles Borromeo looked up from her knitting. "Well, why not? It might do some of us a bit of good to join the real world at last."

"The real world?" said Sister Aloysius. "*The real world*? Might there not be a small theological point at issue here? Or have I taken my vows of poverty, chastity and obedience under a misapprehension?"

"What does the Rev Muv think of this?" asked Sister Mark.

"Oh, Rev Muv's in a blue funk of course. What did you expect? But she's talked about it to some of the others, Sister Monica, Sister Scholastica. I'm surprised you haven't heard already. Sister Monica told me."

"I'm sorry," said Sister Aloysius, "but if they think I'm going to . . . heavens, it was bad enough when they did away with our lovely habits. They'll have us in trousers next."

"I hope so," said Sister Mark. "It would be wonderful to wear jeans on the bike. So what did Sister Scholastica make of the news?"

"Hard to say, isn't it? Sister Scholastica seems to be in an odd mood at the moment. I don't think life's treating her too well just now."

"Poor Sister Scholastica," said Sister Charles Borromeo. "Are her irregular verbs getting out of hand? Her past participles playing her up? Is she losing control of her gerundives?"

"Now, now," said Sister Imelda. "Charity, Sister, charity."

Much later, Carmen awoke with a buzzing ache in her head and a foul mouth. What time was it? Half past one? Oh God, why couldn't she have done the job properly and finish it off once and for all?

The doctor had shaken his head and taken a long time to reply. How long? Weeks? Months? Years? No, my dear, he said, gently, I don't think years. . . .

So, you silly man in a dress, what do you think you can do about that, eh? Just how do you think you can help?

Sister Scholastica met Rachel Gold on the dark corner of the stairs just underneath the statue of Saint Joseph. Rachel looked up smiling until she saw the expression on the nun's face.

"What is it, Sister?"

"Didn't I ask for that Horace unseen to be on my desk first thing?"

Rachel clapped a hand to her mouth, shaking her heavy dark hair. In the dim light shadows defined delicate hollows in her cheek, her neck. Sister Scholastica kept her eyes hard on her.

"Sister, I'm sorry! I forgot all about it. But it'll be there tomorrow, I promise."

"I see. And is that supposed to be a good enough answer?"

"I said I'm sorry."

"So you did."

"I'll do it tonight, I promise." Rachel's brows came together a little pained and surprised. But also, Sister noticed, impatiently too, as if she wanted to be off with her friends.

"Oh, you will, will you? You'll put it off once more just like you put everything else off, I suppose."

"Sister, that's not fair."

"Is it not? It's not fair that I'm supposed to sit around waiting for you to deign to be ready? It's not fair that you have to do the same as everyone else at this school?"

"No, Sister, but . . ."

"Well, I'll tell you what Sister but. You pull your socks up my girl or there'll be no scholarship, no Oxford, no university even. Unless she bucks her ideas up, Miss Rachel Gold will end up working behind a counter in Woolworths. Do you understand?"

"Yes, Sister."

But the look on Rachel Gold's face showed that she did not.

"Go *on*! You're joking."

"I am not."

"Anne Marie Kelly? On the *common*?"

"That's what I heard."

"You're sending me up."

"I am not. Promise."

"Anne Marie *Kelly*!"

"Hallo, you two. Having an interesting gossip?"

"Have you heard this? Do you know what they're saying about Anne Marie Kelly?"

"No. Do tell. Is it dirty?"

Reverend Mother Dymphna sat behind her desk. Her face was

red, plump-cheeked and jolly but the eyes that flickered out from it were pale green, glassy and reptilian. On the polished surface of her desk, groups of chubby china children cuddled and blew kisses at each other; over the glass-fronted bookcase hung the poster that the sixth form had given her last year: 'Life: for best results, follow Maker's instructions.' Reverend Mother had been reading with some incomprehension the autobiography of a famous pop star turned evangelical Christian. What was it, she thought, about non-Catholics that they always made Jesus sound like some particularly efficient laxative?

There was a knock at the door. It was Miss Holt, one of the lay teachers. "I'm sorry to interrupt, Reverend Mother, but there's a story going round that I thought you ought to hear. It's about Anne Marie Kelly, that rather dim little girl in the third year...."

"Can't it wait, Angelina?" asked Rachel. "I'm fearfully tired, and I've got a history essay and a hundred lines of Latin to translate."

"No, Miss Rachel. Is very important."

"Look, if mum's run out of polish again...."

"No, is not the polish. Is more important than the polish."

"Angelina, my head's splitting."

"You listen to me just a minute, Miss Rachel, and then I bring you a nice cup coffee and an aspirin."

"Oh, *Angelina!*"

"No, you listen. You be surprised when you hear. This as big as Lourdes, I think, this as big as Fatima."

"What is, Angelina?"

"Is a miracle, Miss Rachel, that's what is. A real miracle. At least that what I think."

"All right; you tell me."

"Well, Miss Rachel, is that little girl Anne Marie Kelly, who go to your school. Her mother and me we go to the same church, Saint Gertrude's."

"Oh yes, I know Anne Marie. She's in the third year."

"Well, you know what happen to her the other day?"

"What?"

Angelina opened her eyes wide. "Anne Marie Kelly, she see Our Lady!"

Rachel snorted. "Angelina, really!"

"Is God's truth, Miss Rachel, I swear it. Mrs Kelly she tell me the other day. She say her daughter come home and tell her that Our Lady appear to her on the common, just as she on her way home. And Mrs Kelly she say you no telling me truth, Anne Marie, you telling me a big lie. And Anne Marie say I'm not telling no lie, if you don't believe me you come back next week, because Our Lady come back next week and the week after that. So when I see Mrs Kelly in church she say you come with me Angelina when I go to the common with Anne Marie because I think now my girl she telling the truth. So last night we go to the common, and then we wait. And suddenly Anne Marie she fall to her knees on the mud and everything and she start talking. And I swear to you, you could have stick a pin in that girl, Miss Rachel, and she don't notice. 'Yes, no, I do what you want. I brought my mum to see you and Angelina, she a nice friend of my mum.' Honest, Miss Rachel, she say that. And I think, well, I wish Our Lady do something about my leg — you know I tell you about my leg where I have that accident in Italy year before I come here. I tell you, Miss Rachel, that leg is a real bugger. Sometimes I can't get to sleep it go throb throb throb it really hurt me. Only I don't complain, because what's the use complaining? You complain all the time, people they get fed up hearing it. But I'm telling you, Miss Rachel, last night with my leg, I didn't got no pain. The first time, Miss Rachel, since before the accident. That mean Our Lady she must be listening there on the common! Is a miracle, I tell you, a real miracle!"

Chapter 3

Hugo's flat, high above the Chelsea rooftops with their steep gables, twisted chimney stacks and odd little spires and cupolas, was almost like a place in a fairy tale, one of those quaint little wintry towns of narrow streets and ancient beadsmen; especially now, as autumn sun battling with a storm cloud burnished the little tower opposite, it reminded him of the old story he used to love, Gerda and Kay leaning out of their vertiginous windows talking and exchanging secrets before the ice had entered Kay's heart. His flat was right at the top of a tall red house, above the restaurants, the interior designers, the expensive dry cleaners. At night you could barely hear the traffic except as the roar of a distant sea and when he had drawn his curtains and lit the lamps and everything glowed and glittered beneath the sloping eaves, he felt as though he was enclosed in a treasure chamber, a mermaid's or a genie's, somewhere secret and fast and shining.

But doomed too. For next year the lease of this lovely place ran out (he had been living there anyway at an absurdly low rent, having taken it over from an old uncle who'd gone into a home), and then he would be cast out into the world. Friends told him of places like Muswell Hill and Tooting Bec, where they said perfectly nice flats could be found, but he shuddered at the thought. Only a real fairy tale would save him now. Was there perhaps a genie's lamp amongst his treasures?

The doorbell buzzed, startling and worrying him. His meal — a chicken piece with lemon and tarragon, and a jacket potato — crackled away in the oven. Just enough wine remained in the opened bottle in the fridge door to give him a glass and a half with his meal. Perhaps it would be someone selling double glazing who could be quickly despatched.

It was Antonia. She stood there in the doorway with the smell of the cold autumn street upon her and her breath in a mist. She wore a shaggy sheepskin jerkin over a huge soft turquoise sweater and long blue suede boots, to which scraps of orange leaves had stuck. She strode in, pulling off gloves like a cavalry officer in a bad opera. When she put the gloves on the hall table, she also paused to straighten an ornament. Hugo did not think it had needed straightening. Her mass of expensively dishevelled hair stood out around her face. She was a handsome girl — but Hugo was only interested in handsome girls. He could see no point in a plain one.

"Darling, the Hendersons have asked us to the country on Friday. Can we go?"

The statement, with its subtle array of implications, startled him. "*You* can go if you want to."

"They've asked *us*."

"Us?" he said. "There is you, and there is I, but there is not, is there, *us*?"

She sighed and then smiled archly. She was used to his tricky ways. "All right, darling. Let me rephrase it. The Hendersons have asked *me* to the country. They have also asked *you*. I would like to go. I will go. Can you go? Will you go? Will you go with me in the car, if you go? There. Is that better?"

Well, it was a bit. And it wasn't nice to sulk. "I'll think about it," he said. In fact he would quite like to say yes. Antonia's social life bristled with good connections. The Hendersons' house was seventeenth-century and had been built over the ruins of a convent. It had even, so they said, its own ghost — one of those ubiquitous nuns walled up for having a love affair.

"Why don't we go to the pub," said Antonia, "and you can make up your mind over a vodka and tonic?"

"I was hoping to do some work," he said, putting reproof into his voice.

"Oh, I haven't come to seduce you from your work!" Her

voice swooped huskily. "Just half an hour, I can't stay anyway. I'm on my way to Sophie's."

She could never stay, Antonia. Friends beckoned and begged and insisted. '*Darling*! Lovely to hear . . . No, not this evening, I'm busy. Look, what about . . . Oh, are you? *Wonderful*! Listen, why don't you come round tomorrow? I'm so pleased for you, my angel. Must dash. Oh, nine-ish. Lovely! *Ciao*!' Her own flat was like a hotel, a box to contain only a small part of her life. To Hugo his flat was part of himself. He loved to come home at night and draw the curtains knowing that he did not have to go out again, relishing his solitude.

Should they go to the pub? The Duke of Clarence with the hearties? The King's Head with the pooves? There was a nice bottle of Saint-Emilion in the cupboard that Lady Bathmaker had brought. Should he open it or save it for a more important occasion? "Let's have a drink here, shall we?" he said. Adding pointedly, "Wait a moment while I turn the oven down." Antonia shrugged. His subtle self-sacrifices were lost on her. She followed him into the kitchen.

"How's the writing going?"

"Not bad." He heard the defensiveness in his voice and rephrased it. "Quite well actually."

"Good," she said. "By the way, I've got a vision for you myself. It was one of the things I came over to tell you."

"You've got. . . ?" he questioned, bending over the fridge door to see if the *Gewürztraminer* would possibly stretch to two glasses. It would not.

"A vision, darling. Vision! V-i-s-i-o-n. The real thing, apparently."

"What do you mean?"

"Have I ever told you about my nice friend Mr Gold? He's a little Jew from Surbiton or Streatham or somewhere." Antonia was one of those well-bred English people who could spit out the word 'Jew' as though it were some peculiarly distasteful half-digested mouthful.

"No, I don't think so."

"Are you sure? I must have done. He's rather a sweetie, actually. He's an accountant or a surveyor or something. His wife's a very high-powered doctor somewhere and he has this amazing daughter who is not only the greatest genius the world has ever known since Albert Einstein but beautiful to boot. You know how Jews go on. Anyway, my Mr Gold wants to be cultured, so he comes to see me in the gallery and we have little chats about Lowry. And I advise him what would go with his gold flock wallpaper. I don't actually know whether he's got gold flock wallpaper, but I wouldn't be surprised if he has. Jews never have taste, do they? I wonder why that is? You'd think they'd be artistic, wouldn't you?"

A small liberal voice inside Hugo felt it ought to raise a protest and he opened his mouth to suggest Chagall and Modigliani, but she waved him into silence. "All right, darling, you know perfectly well what I mean, you don't have to lecture me. Now where was I? Oh yes, Mr Gold came into the gallery this morning." Antonia, who had private means, drifted from one pleasant inconsequential job to another. At present she worked in a Bond Street art gallery which marketed Art as an Investment. "Anyway we had our little chat, and I told him that Balthus was fearfully good news these days and he said how interesting, it was time they bought a painting anyway, and then I asked him how the Infant Phenomenon was getting along, and then he told me this funny story. . . . Darling, you're not opening a bottle specially are you? I'm not even sure if I've got time. Well, just a drop."

"I'm afraid it's still a bit chilled," he said. "Warm it in your hands." It was *very* good Saint-Emilion. He should have saved it.

"Oh, I like it a bit cold," she said, taking a gulp. "Anyway, Charles says we all drink red wine too warm in England. The Frogs often chill it, you know."

"The Frogs do terrible things to wine," he said sternly. "They have so much they can afford to."

"By the way, do you want to go shares on a crate of the new Beaujolais when it comes? Charles is hoping to grab some from this friend of his who runs — I told you, didn't I — that wine bar in the Fulham Road. I said I'd ask if you were interested."

"I'm not," he said.

"I can't see the point either myself; it tastes just like paint stripper to me. But you know Charles. *Do* you know Charles, by the way? No, perhaps you don't. No thanks, no more. I was telling you a story."

"About Mr Gold."

"That's right. Well, the Golds have this Italian housekeeper. And she claims that there's a local girl who's been having visions of the Virgin Mary."

"Darling, the loony bins are full of people like that."

"Yes, but this one's different, apparently."

"They always are."

She smiled at him. "Come, come. I thought you had to believe in all this stuff."

"Stuff, Antonia?"

"You know, visions and miracles and all that. I thought it went with the set."

"Far from it, actually. In fact the official view of the church is quite austere. It's popular acclaim that makes places like Lourdes and Fatima so famous."

"Darling, you're lecturing me again. All I was saying was that you might, if pushed, think it not absolutely impossible that the Virgin Mary just might come down to earth for a little chat now and then."

"I might. But I'd have to be pushed pretty hard."

"Darling, if you can believe, and you do because you told me you had to, that Jesus sent his poor little Jewish mother zooming up to the skies without a spacesuit, then you can jolly well listen to Angelina's vision."

"All right then, I'll listen."

"Apparently, Angelina, that's the housekeeper, went along with the girl and the girl's mother to see what happened. And Angelina asked the Virgin to cure some pain she has in her leg, and the Virgin obliged. Hey presto! A miracle!"

"Did Angelina see the vision too?"

"No. Nobody does, except the little girl. She's called Anne Marie, I think. There, wasn't it good of me to remember all that?"

"How old is the girl?"

"Oh I don't know. Twelve, thirteen, something like that. They always are, aren't they? Like poltergeists. There's always a mad adolescent girl about."

"Antonia, you watch too many horror films. Well, it's an interesting story all right, but I don't suppose there's anything in it."

"Of course there isn't anything in it! You know perfectly well, or at least you don't because you're a silly Catholic otherwise you would, that there isn't anything in the whole business! I'm just telling you what I heard. I thought it might be useful. I won't bother you next time."

"No, I'm very grateful really. It was nice of you to take an interest. But . . ."

"But?"

"This isn't really the kind of vision that I had in mind. I can't quite see how I can make use of it."

"Oh, I see. It's not as good as Saint Thingummy and her fiery sword, I suppose."

"No, darling, it's not that."

"Or that Saint Fatty person. I suppose that was better, was it?"

"Darling girl, Fatima is a place not a person. But that's not the point. I mean a certain sort of vision is quite common. I'm interested in the ones that aren't."

"I don't understand you. You want visions, I find you a vision."

"I've just told you."

"You want dead visions, don't you? You want to do it all in books. You don't want to get up off your Catholic arse and talk to somebody who's actually *had* a vision, do you?"

"The girl's probably a lunatic."

"I'm sure she is. But that's the difference between us, isn't it? I *know* they're all lunatics, you think that some of them just might not be. The problem is which? If I were you, I'd at least want to go and find out."

Once Antonia got an idea into her head, she never let go. Of course she could hardly be expected to understand the finer points of his theory, but on the other hand, maybe she wasn't altogether wrong about this one. "Well . . . I don't know. Perhaps."

"Perhaps! *Perhaps!* Hugo, you are so slippery! But I love you." Antonia never sulked for long. "And sweetie, do say yes to the Hendersons and we can have a lovely snuggly weekend together."

"I might, I'll see."

"There! I knew you would. Now just listen to me about nice Mr Gold's housekeeper too and you'll be my favourite person." She cast a glance at the fur hearthrug before the fire. "I say, darling, I've got ten minutes. What say we take a look at your fiery sword?"

"You mustn't think of God as a vindictive sort of fellow," said Father Joyce, "though many people see Him as one. He doesn't heap troubles on people's heads just to see how well they bear up. God's a rational being. We know that because we are made in His image and we're rational beings too."

Were we? Was He? And did anyone care? Father Joyce hated sermons; he hated the sense of being a schoolmaster instructing a naughty class. Nothing was ever said that had not been said a hundred, nay a thousand, times before and nobody listened.

Nobody listened in Saint Gertrude's this morning. He could have taken a bet on it. That old girl in the front row looked as though she was taking in every word, but she was deaf as a post. Further back young Kevin Kelly seemed to be doing something terrible with his hymn book, and the pretty Portuguese au pair from Elmwood Drive knew hardly a word of English. Also in the front row, upright and smiling encouragingly, was Mr Painscastle. Well, perhaps Mr Painscastle was listening. But Mr

Painscastle did all the right things. Father Joyce hoped God found him boring too. Otherwise the prospect of sharing eternal bliss with Mr Painscastle was almost enough to put you off. Next to Mr Painscastle sat nice Sister Mahony. Sister Mahony, from a more democratic order of nuns than those of the Seven Sorrows, wore a navy blue suit with a small gold cross round her neck. Father Joyce had mixed feelings about the ladies of the Seven Sorrows — they were not actually in his parish, but their boundaries nudged so closely that some contact was inevitable. For their parts, the Seven Sorrows nuns were always coolly polite to him, while they enthused in warm tones about his predecessor, Father Ross, a venerable-looking man with thick silver hair and a fierce belief in hellfire and original sin, whose sermons against birth control had been so violent that anybody with a family of fewer than six children was frightened to come to church.

Presumably Father Ross would have approved of the Kellys, who spread out over an entire pew: little Mrs Kelly who had once been pretty and was no longer, lumpy Anne Marie, Lisa, Kevin the horror, and the twins, Dermot and Steven. They were a sprawling untidy family and scarcely a Sunday passed without a Kelly getting up to some mischief or other. But today there was something different about them. Mrs Kelly had never looked so smart. A hat sat jauntily on her auburn curls and there was a scarf around her neck. Anne Marie wore her school uniform and a black lace mantilla, and on her puddingy face there was an expression of trepidation, a sort of self-conscious public look that he had never seen there before.

Kevin Kelly turned round in his pew and appeared to be flicking pieces of paper (torn from the Westminster Hymnal?) at the old black lady in the seat behind. If the Kellys had not been there, the church would have looked half empty. . . .

He began to lose his train of thought. "God does not . . . God does not . . ." What had he been going to say? God does not like you to use Mrs Owolowu for target practice, Kevin Kelly? God does really not, Mr Painscastle, want to hear your theories on the nature of life yet again. God does not want you, His people, to sit through His service with that look of utter boredom on your faces. But a priest must tread a safe path. "God does not," he said, "like it when his children refuse to use those gifts he has given them, those precious gifts of common sense and reason. We are to walk boldly, not stumble blindly. We have been given only one life on this earth, my dear people. Let us not sleep it away. That's all for now. The Bishop asks me to tell you that there will be a collection for our mission in the Falkland Islands at the end of the service. Please give what you can. In the name of the Father and of the Son and of the Holy Ghost. . . ."

Carmen hoped she would oversleep, but no such luck; she was awake at half past seven. She felt awful, but then of course she would, wouldn't she? Since she was awake perhaps she ought to get some canvasses together and go to the railings in time to get her pitch. If she wasn't careful, that horrible Ron with the woolly dogs would grab it. Honest Ron, the artists called him disdainfully.
    Oh hell. Honest Ron was welcome to it.
    Sod the railings.
    Sod art.
    Sod life, or what was left of it.
    Time for a drink soon. Go on.

Rachel was quite enjoying her Sunday. Sundays, being devoted to family visiting, had their own sort of pressure, but it was a relief to get away from Sin and Grace and Sacrifice and it was a relief — it was a special relief — to get away from Sister Scholastica. Her grandmother lived in Hendon, in a flat that glittered with tiny exquisite objects. Grandmother went to the synagogue dutifully, but the chief gods she recognised seemed to reside in hairdressers' salons and department stores. Then there were the cousins, of assorted degrees of genius, to hear about. It drove her mother mad sometimes, but for Rachel it was a soothing alternative world, where she could for once throw off all her problems and be a child again, pampered and adored.

Well, at last there was somebody sitting in his little room. "Father, I have to talk to you," Mrs Kelly had said at the end of Mass and now the room was overflowing with Kellys. They fidgeted and giggled and infused the air with a faint smell of dirty knees. Mr Painscastle had somehow got in on the act too, and had taken the chair opposite Mrs Kelly, leaving Father Joyce perched uncomfortably on the coffee table. Anne Marie sat on the arm of her mother's chair, keeping her eyes on the floor as though what was happening had nothing to do with her. A few years ago Mrs Kelly might have played the Maureen O'Hara part, running barefoot in a green dress through grass wet with rainbow dew, but the years had not been kind to her, the little mouth had set hard and the Irish eyes turned to stainless steel. In her diminutive hand she clutched a custard cream biscuit; she looked at Father Joyce as though she wished it were his throat.

"You don't believe me, do you?"

Father Joyce sought a diplomatic way of saying no. "It's not that, Mrs Kelly, it's just . . ."

"No," said Mrs Kelly, "you don't believe me." She gave an odd little satisfied laugh.

"We would be failing in our duty. . . ." said Mr Painscastle. The royal 'we' came naturally to him.

"I knew you wouldn't believe me," said Mrs Kelly.

"It's a lot to take in," said the priest. "Why don't you let Anne Marie tell the story in her own words?"

Anne Marie looked up in horror. "Don't you intimidate her now," said Mrs Kelly.

"Mum," said Dermot Kelly suddenly, "can I go to the toilet?"

"Lisa, take your brother to the toilet. And see he washes his hands after."

"Second door to the left at the end of the corridor," said Father Joyce.

"Oh ye of little faith," said Mrs Kelly. "Didn't I tell you, Anne Marie, didn't I tell you he wouldn't believe you?"

"Aren't you being a little unfair, Mrs Kelly?" interposed Mr Painscastle. "After all, you've hardly given Father a chance."

"Walk boldly, not stumble blindly," said Mrs Kelly. "Isn't that what you said yourself? Now here's the greatest thing you'll ever hear and you've got your eyes shut."

"I really would like to hear it from Anne Marie herself," said Father Joyce, "before you accuse me of all sorts of things."

Mrs Kelly looked at Anne Marie, who was wiggling her toes over the faded pattern in the carpet, and suddenly she had a change of heart. "Lisa," she said as the girl reappeared in the doorway, "take the little ones downstairs and wait for me there. And make sure they don't go near that road."

"Can I have some sweets, Mum?" said Kevin.

"No, you may not. Do you want all your teeth to fall out?"

Slowly the room emptied of Kellys. The smell of dirty knees hung in the air, vaguely reproachful.

"Right," said their mother. "Now tell the Father."

Anne Marie still looked at the floor. "I serraisaura, din I?" she said to the carpet.

"Speak up now, Anne Marie. Do you think the Father's going to eat you?" said Mrs Kelly. She looked at Father Joyce as though she thought him quite capable of it.

Anne Marie's remark when elucidated proved scarcely worth the trouble of waiting for. "I said I saw her, didn't it?"

"Do you think I believed her the first time she said it? Do you think I'm so gullible I take in a story like that straight away?" Mrs Kelly's vocabulary seemed to expand in little disconcerting bursts. "Didn't I threaten to beat the living daylights out of her for her presumption the first time she came home bare-faced and told me? Didn't I, Anne Marie?"

Anne Marie nodded.

"Then I must ask you, Mrs Kelly," said Father Joyce, "what made you change your mind and decide she was telling the truth?"

"You come there," said Mrs Kelly firmly. "You just come to the common and watch my Anne Marie when Our Blessed Lady appears. You wouldn't doubt then, I promise you."

Chapter 4

Hugo's weekend was a disaster. "Don't tell me, *Ample*forth!" shrieked a large girl with a big chin across the dinner table. And, "Darling Hugo," said Sally Henderson, who was having a bad time with her husband, "come and sit next to me and tell me how pretty I'm looking." Moreover it was raining and dozens of daffodil bulbs were to be planted. "Jump to it, peasants!" called Sally, standing in the warm doorway with a huge apron and a gin and tonic. "Drinkies all round when you've finished!" while Hugo, who had worn a good suit, scrabbled in the wet ground.

The house may have been seventeenth-century but the Henderson's taste, which ran to brocade suites and carriage lamps, most decidedly was not. "See Maples and die," whispered another house guest, a camp interior designer who had taken quite a shine to Hugo. Sally's cooking showed few traces of the cordon bleu course she had once taken, except for a penchant for cutting lemons into waterlilies, and Antonia was in one of her satirical and enigmatic moods. Sally had bedded them together without asking which was annoying too. Hugo did not like arrangements to be taken for granted; and Antonia was an irritating person to spend an entire night with as she sprawled over three quarters of the bed. And then just as he was in the act of making love to her, his bottom most inelegantly exposed, a beam of light at the door and a loud clanking noise announced Don Henderson, clad in a white sheet and doing his usual weekend joke of pretending to be the ghost nun. Afterwards Hugo tried to return to the business of pleasuring Antonia, but it was no good, and had gone irredeemably limp and Antonia, past the point of no return, became sulky and fractious with him, quite unfairly,

Hugo thought when it was she who had such silly friends.

Sunday was the local thirteenth-century church where, they said, the services were so High Hugo would hardly be able to tell the difference. "I'm sure even the Pope wouldn't notice," said Sally.

The church was very fine with some good effigies and an only partly damaged rood screen, but the vicar with his benign smile and plummy establishment voice did not convince him for a moment. In all Anglican services, he felt, there was something missing. Everything was too polite, too moderated. There was no space for rapture in a religion that was primarily about good manners. And it was an uncomfortable feeling to know that his own religion lurked in the bones of the little church and rightfully belonged there; almost certainly a violent vision of hell was hidden beneath the plain white walls and Mrs Fortescue's tasteful arrangement of honesty and bulrush heads. "I do look forward to seeing you all at the Bring and Buy Sale," said the vicar. "There," said Sally afterwards, "no difference at all. Didn't I tell you he was a sweetie? Now who's going to volunteer for spud bashing?" Hugo arrived home on Sunday evening with a headache and a plastic carrier bag of windfalls, most of them maggoty.

Sister Scholastica had not enjoyed her weekend either. They were distempering the downstairs corridor which always brought on her allergy and she had been finding sleep very difficult these last weeks anyway. The nuns' rooms were only thinly partitioned; if she switched a light on, she would wake Sister Louis on one side and Sister Walpurgis on the other. In the old days, the days of the strict rule, it would have been lights out at ten and no two ways about it; now she had the spiritual liberty to read in bed, but not the practical. So she lay there, arms outside the bedclothes in the way she had been taught when she first came to the convent, staring at the grey bumpy ceiling and trying to banish inappropriate thoughts from her mind.

But the thoughts *would* come! A thousand demons using the inside of her head like a cinder track! If the other sisters only knew!

There is no soundness in my flesh because of Thy indignation, there is no health in my bones because of my sin. . . .

As you struggled it got worse, but what else could you do against vileness but struggle?

. . . for my iniquities have gone over my head, they weigh like a burden too heavy for me. . . .

How she longed to be *good*, perfect and hard and pure as a piece of crystal.

But just as she was finally about to fall asleep, there came suddenly into her mind a picture of Rachel Gold, smiling gently beneath her halo of bronze-black hair. . . .

"Honestly, it gives you indigestion just to *look* at her," said Sister Mark.

"I was sure I'd beat her into chapel this morning," whispered Sister Louis, "so I got there very early, but no, there she was kneeling on the floor. And then she turned round and told me to make less noise. Just as though I were a first-former!"

"At breakfast she told me not to bolt my cornflakes; like a greedy child, she said."

"Oh, that's nothing, my dear Sisters," said Sister Charles Borromeo. "Did you hear my coughing fit at Vespers yesterday? Well she told me if I was ill I should be in the infirmary and not spoiling other people's concentration."

"If you ask me, she's going round the bend," said Sister Mark.

"Sit down there, dear," said Reverend Mother. When Reverend Mother said 'dear' it meant trouble. Anne Marie, her face expressionless, sat down. There was food on her school blazer and her dingy shirt had the kind of pressed-in creases that result from too much careless launderetting. Reverend Mother believed strongly in what she called 'the nicer type of girl'. Today her gnome face simmered darkly across the polished table. Anne Marie did not, would not, look her in the eyes.

"I think you know why I've called you here," said Reverend Mother.

"Yes, Reverend Mother."

"Speak up, child!" Though in fact in the stillness of Reverend Mother's room, Anne Marie's voice was perfectly audible.

"Yes, Reverend Mother," she repeated at exactly the same decibel level as before.

"Well?"

"What, Reverend Mother?"

"What, Reverend Mother? *What*, Reverend Mother? I want to hear the truth behind these ridiculous rumours, that's what, Reverend Mother."

"I told the truth, Reverend Mother."

"I very much doubt that, Anne Marie. I very much doubt that indeed."

"I did though," said the girl sulkily.

"Very well then. Let's see if I've got it right. You say, forgive me if I'm mistaken, that Our Blessed Lady had the goodness to appear to you, Anne Marie Kelly, on the common, one evening, after school."

"Three times, Reverend Mother."

"I beg your pardon?"

"It's three times now, Reverend Mother, she came again on Thursday."

"Oh, pardon me, I'm very sorry. You're saying that Our Blessed Lady has appeared to you three times on the common."

"Yes, Reverend Mother."

"To *you*, Anne Marie Kelly of IIIA?"

"Yes, Reverend Mother."

"Why should she want to do that, do you suppose?"

"I don't know, Reverend Mother."

"On the *common*! A place where people exercise their dogs and all sort of . . . a place like *that*?"

"I don't know, Reverend Mother."

"Oh do stop repeating 'I don't know, Reverend Mother' like a demented parrot! It's time you did know. I want an explanation. Why should *Our Lady* choose to appear to you?"

"I don't . . ." For a second Anne Marie looked up. A brief fire blazed in her eyes. "She appeared to Bernadette, didn't she?"

"Bernadette was a *saint*, child."

"Not when she first saw her she wasn't."

"Are you comparing yourself with *Saint Bernadette*?"

"No, but . . ."

"What then?"

"I don't know, Reverend Mother."

"I should think not indeed. Saint Bernadette! Well, I hope you'll go away from here and say a little prayer to God to forgive you for your cheek. In fact I think it may have to be quite a big prayer, don't you, Anne Marie? You're going to have to ask His forgiveness for . . ." Reverend Mother broke off in mid-sentence to examine Anne Marie, who still sat impassive, plump little knees bulging white beneath her skirt, fingers arranged stiffly on her lap, ". . . for telling lies, Anne Marie."

"I'm not telling no lies," said the girl sullenly.

"Forgive me, Anne Marie, but I think you are. I think you made up the whole silly story just to draw attention to yourself. Now, admit that I'm right."

Anne Marie shook her head.

"Pardon?" said the nun.

"I did see her," said Anne Marie. "My mum believes me."

"Oh, your *mum* believes you. And that makes it all all right, does it, your mum believes you. Well, let me tell you, I'm not so easily persuaded as your mum. I don't believe you. I want to find a good reason why Our Lady should choose to appear to you, and quite frankly, so far I haven't.

"She'll tell me."

"She being the cat's mother, I assume?"

"Our Lady."

"Oh, I see. Our Lady hasn't yet deigned to tell you why she's come but she will one day, is that it?"

"Not one day. Soon."

"Oh you must be looking forward to that, Anne Marie."

"Yes, Reverend Mother."

"It must be very gratifying to you that out of all the girls in the school, indeed out of all the girls in the world, out of all the *people* in the world, out of all the *holy* people in the world . . . like Cardinal Hume, like Mother Teresa, like His Holiness himself, it is to *Anne Marie Kelly* alone that Our Blessed Lady, Queen of Heaven, will reveal her message. I hope you feel honoured."

"Yes, Reverend Mother."

Really, it was like addressing a piece of school rice pudding! "*Yes, Reverend Mother,*" she mimicked. "For goodness' sake, Anne Marie, do you take me for a complete fool?"

But all Anne Marie would say to that was, "I did see her. I'm not going to say I didn't."

Rachel leaned out of her bedroom window. Before her, inky black and silent, ridged with waves like a fossilised sea, its mysteries concealed by the snarl of brambles and thorns that divided it from the roadside, was the common. The sky was an extraordinary colour, a luminous, intense Disneyland blue, and out of it shone a huge moon. Hunter's Moon? Harvest Moon? It was so big and calm and bright, spreading its halo around and lighting up the trees and the common like a silver pencil. She never used to believe in moonlight; she thought it was just a word. It was so beautiful. Life should be beautiful, and yet. . . . Sometimes she could *scream*. The pressure inside her built up like air in a balloon and soon, she felt, the balloon must burst. Oh God, God. It was all so terrible, and yet . . . exciting too. What was she so excited about? Her body vibrated like a twanged harp string. All that moonlight. It was so *unfair*. Here she was, forced to be a schoolgirl, in an ordinary house, when all around, there was . . . moonlight, and things like that. She wanted—what did she want? She wanted a share in all the excitement that must be going on somewhere. She wanted to be *different*, she wanted to escape from the pattern that was being laid down for her by her parents. God, if she thought she'd end up like them, she'd *die*. Would she go on forever, being fussed over at home and bullied by Sister Scholastica?

If only she *knew*. If only she knew what she wanted.

Chapter 5

My acclaimed faith makes me suffer, the young man leaning languidly against a bramble-snarled tree was saying. Or rather, that was what was spelled out by the gilt motto over his head. But the young man in the Hilliard miniature did not seem to be suffering very much at all, or if he was, he put on a remarkably brave face. Hugo had placed him there that morning, propped up next to David on his desk, but there was something about the picture that made him feel even more uneasy than did David's sexual ambiguity. *Dat poenas laudata fides*; his faith *did* make him suffer, there was no doubt about it, though he did not imagine that the young Elizabethan aristocrat, nor indeed anyone else, would be wildly sympathetic towards his sufferings. If it was not quite yet the dark night of his soul, it was certainly some time towards its late afternoon.

He would not have admitted it, even to himself, but his interest in the medieval mystics had begun ever so slightly to wane. If he had hoped that by reading them he might come to share their transports, that he would know the faith that ravished the soul, he was disappointed. After all this time, he had only a sense of being a spectator on the outside of a glass case. Behind the glass they moved and mouthed and gestured, but he could never quite hear what they were saying. Moreover, as they starved and beat themselves, saw legions of devils, anguished about sin and walled themselves up (how smelly Dame Julian must have been) he could not help but feel that they weren't, any of them, quite the sort of people one wanted to know.

In the middle of the morning, the telephone rang. It was his agent, full of enthusiasm. He had just come from a conversation with the editor of a large paperback firm who had shown great interest in the idea of Hugo's book; religion was suddenly chic again, apparently. The only problem was that the book which his agent had described had very little to do with the book Hugo thought he was writing. The editor, it seemed, was an amateur psychologist and knew his stuff: visions were what happened when adolescent girls were sexually repressed. Hugo started to protest — this sort of titillation was exactly what he was trying to avoid — but his agent cut him short by mentioning the sum of money the editor had in mind for an advance. It was larger than anything Hugo had ever earned in his life before and he stopped protesting, quite breathless. Silkily the agent continued. "Ghastly, isn't it, but that's the way of the world these days, and you surely don't want to write yet another book that no one's going to read."

That 'yet another' cut deep. Whilst he smarted, his agent said, "A good read for the man on the Clapham omnibus and all that. I know you can do it, Hugo. Give it a go."

The phone rang again almost immediately afterwards and he picked it up in the certainty that it was his agent ringing to apologise for his unkindness in reminding Hugo about that last book, but it was his mother.

"Well, you were obviously standing close to the phone," she said. "I thought you'd be buried deep in your books."

"Mother," he said with dignity, "I've just been talking to my agent." Dignity did not travel well down telephone wires. He could hear her light little giggle. "Well, that's your story, darling, and you're sticking to it. Now listen. I shall be in town this morning; I have some shopping to do and I'm meeting Janet for lunch. Will you be home at three?"

"Yes, I think so," he said, trying to sound as though there might be many calls on his time that day.

"Good. Then I shall come and see you. We can have a cup of your extremely smart tea and you can have a good moan at me if you want. Three o'clock then."

"Yes, Mother," he said, but the phone had clicked down before he had finished saying it. He peered disconsolately into the purring earpiece as though she could somehow be recalled and redirected.

Some mornings could never be rescued. He put on his coat and went out. In Sloane Avenue, he turned towards Knightsbridge.

Mother was odd, there was no doubt about that, and she was becoming odder. It was since his father died that her eccentricities had become embarrassing; before that, she had merely smoked too much and talked too loudly at school functions. Now she did not smoke at all and had taken up various strange eastern religions. Other people's mothers baked cakes and had their faces lifted; Hugo's went to courses on meditation and hung mandalas on her walls. It was not what you expected of a mother who ought to be there soothing the more difficult times of your life. As a small child, he remembered he had been entranced by her, and what seemed to be the mysteries of her daily routine. Dazzled, he had watched as she opened jars and bottles, swooningly scented, and dabbed and patted and puffed. She hung pale pearls in her ears and draped glowing topazes around her neck. Buried deep in her drawers were objects she would not talk about. When he asked questions she smiled and said, "You'll understand when you're older, my love." He thought it was a promise, not yet recognising a put-off.

Mysteries, mysteries. How the world had glimmered and glowed with them in those days; so many things spoken of only in whispers, or not at all, so many things unexplained and unknown. Yet the years passed, he had acquired education, should know the answers. But it seemed to him that he understood less than ever, and the mysteries — different ones now — were still there. Would there ever be a time when the world shone clear as glass?

Mother was late, of course. "Goodness, Hugo, you do make such a fuss about punctuality. It's not healthy, you know. What is that extraordinary thing on your mantelpiece?"

"It's a William de Morgan vase, Mother."

"Wonderful. My Aunt May had a house full of things like that. We threw them all out when she died. Not even the junk shop wanted them. You *are* looking pale, dear. Are you well?"

"Mother, I am perfectly well. Stop trying to reduce me to size. Let me take this horse blanket from you."

"Poncho, darling. It's called a poncho. I'm sure you know that. I've worn it for years."

"I haven't seen you for years."

"Oh Hugo, how you exaggerate."

"Months, then."

"Well, whose fault is that? You never come to see me any more."

"You never come to see me either."

As she arched her eyebrows, her pale, scrubbed, freckled English face, with its slightly surprised expression, mirrored his own. He always felt a little violated at this appropriation of his features — his face, he thought, should have been for his own exclusive use. Especially now, the figure she cut in flowing Indian cottons and hand-knitted sweaters (make-up and glittery jewellery had long since vanished from the scene) represented all sorts of things with which he preferred not to be associated.

"Learn to drive," she said. "Then we could see each other more often."

"*You* learn to drive," said Hugo. "You know perfectly well I can't afford a car."

"You poor starving dear! Well, what about a cup of tea? Can you afford that, do you think?"

"I can even afford some cake with it. Would you like a piece?"

"What sort?"

"Harrods, Dundee."

"Only the merest fraction, then. I'm on this marvellous new diet . . . but no, we can't talk about diets, can we? Silly Mother and her cranky ways."

"Do you know what you'll have if you eat with me tonight? Veal escalopes. Little slivers of anaemic flesh peeled from blind baby calves."

"Oh yes, mock on, mock on. But I can't stay with you anyway. I must catch the train at six. I'll send you a pamphlet I have about intensive farming methods, and I promise you, you'll never joke about a piece of veal again."

"Do stay. It's not veal anyway. That was a tease, as well you know. I've got some plaice. Nice fresh plaice. I went to Harrods this morning."

"I thought you were supposed to be so busy writing."

"You can't sit writing all day. It's not like an office job. Sometimes you have to breathe, to let the air get to you."

"So when you want the air to get to you, you go to *Harrods*?" Mother pulled a wry face.

"Harrods is my nearest decent shop. You make such a thing of it."

"All those Tory ladies matching buttons."

"It's not like that any more."

"Well, I must say, I'm glad to be out of it. How *is* the writing going?"

"Not too bad, thank you," he lied.

"You know, I wish you'd write another of your novels. I quite enjoyed the last one."

"*Quite enjoyed*," said Hugo between gritted teeth. "Thank you, Mother. There. Take your tea."

"Cups and saucers!" said Mother. "I haven't used a saucer for years."

"I know. You have those ghastly grindy mugs."

"They're very beautiful mugs. Hand-thrown; Alex makes them specially for me. So when are you going to come and visit me again?"

"What about the weekend after next?"

"No, not that weekend. That weekend, I'm away on a residential course on Sufism."

"Really! At your age."

"One is never too old," she said, "for growth. One sugar, please. I shouldn't take it, but it's a habit I can't break."

"I think you're being a teeny bit ridiculous."

"Then think it, my dear, it doesn't worry me."

"All those peculiar people. I don't know how you can stand it."

"There are some very peculiar people in your church too. I remember a most unsalubrious priest who used to have his eye on you. And just because I believe in meditation, it doesn't mean I'm going to walk down Oxford Street with a bald head going jingle jangle. You ought to try meditation, you know. I believe it would do you some good."

"Mother, it's crazy. By the way, do you like this cake?"

"This cake? Dear boy, you are changing the subject. Yes, this cake seems most pleasant."

"Actually, it isn't Harrods. It's Mr Kipling. I thought if I told you that first, you might imagine it was full of chemicals."

"You know," she said, looking at her plate, "sometimes you can be a very *silly* boy. I wish you'd find a nice girlfriend."

"The cure for all ills, a nice girlfriend! Anyway, I have a nice girlfriend at the moment. Antonia is a nice girlfriend."

"Antonia. Now tell me, do I like Antonia?"

"How should I know? You've certainly met her."

"Antonia. Antonia. Short black hair and Woolworth's earrings?"

"No, Mother, that was Kate. Kate was years ago."

"Ah, yes, I remember now. A big girl. Rather good-looking, if you like that sort of thing. *Do* you?"

"Of course. I'm rather fond of Antonia."

"Ah! Then do we hear wedding bells?"

Perhaps Mother was not so different from other mothers after all. "Really, you are being just a little . . ."

"I do long to meet my grandchildren before I go gaga."

"Then, fortunately, I've many years left before I need to think about producing them."

"Mmm," she said, in an unsatisfied tone. And then, "You know, you worry me Hugo."

"I *worry* you?"

"Yes, it's just . . ." She gazed at the ceiling for a moment and then turned her inquisitive birdlike gaze full in his direction.

"Now do tell me. You can be quite honest with me, Hugo. You aren't . . . you aren't a *homosexual*, are you?"

"Mother!"

"Well, are you? You can tell me, you know."

"I think I liked it better before you became enlightened."

"I do still care about you. After all, you are my only son."

"And you, Mother, are my only mother. Thank God."

"You still haven't answered my question."

"No, I am not a homosexual. Is that all right?"

"Are you sure?"

"Well, what proof do you want? Shall I ask Antonia round so you can watch us fornicate?"

"Fornicate," she said musingly, "what a lovely word. I love that word, fornicate. But you see, I can't help thinking it's a little strange, Hugo. A young man like you living like this."

"Like what, for heaven's sake?"

Her eyes swept round the little cluttered tasteful room, missing nothing, the miniatures, the lustre teacups, the collection of ivory boxes, the embroidered cushion covers. Finally her glance came to rest on David and the love-struck Elizabethan youth. The look she gave from beneath her eyelashes was almost as coy as David's own. "Like this," she said.

Chapter 6

"Good-oh," said Mr Painscastle, who seemed to have taken things over. "Are we all here?"

They certainly were. Mrs Kelly's tiny living room seemed to bulge and swell with them, knocking elbows and knees and legs, and trying not to trip over Kevin, Dermot and Steven who were intent on watching the television through everything. Angelina was there, and Sister Mahony, as was Mrs Markinowski from next door, and Linda Markinowski, who thought the whole thing was silly if you asked her (nobody did, though), Mr Blackaby who suffered from migraines, Mrs Evans-Blow, Miss Finch and Mr Thomson who had come down for the occasion from the South London Friends of Fatima Association. None of them had ever been present at a vision before and no one knew quite how to behave. Mrs Evans-Blow made nervous jokes while Miss Finch fingered her rosary.

But all fell quiet for little Mrs Kelly, who came into the room dressed in her Sunday best. "Very well," she said, surveying the scene. "Anne Marie should be down soon. Lisa . . . Lisa, where are you? I'm leaving you in charge of the little ones, and Dermot, if you touch that trifle before I get back I'll kill you, do you understand?"

"Can I go out and get some crisps, Mum?" said Kevin.

"You may certainly not. You stay in that chair or I'll want to know the reason why. Now has anyone got a card they'd like to give Anne Marie?"

"A card?" asked Mrs Markinowski.

"Didn't they tell you? What we do," said Mrs Kelly, as though they had been doing it for weeks, "is to write down on a postcard any petitions we have for Our Lady, and then hand them over to Anne Marie who shows them to her."

"Do we write in English?" quavered Miss Finch, who wanted to put in a plea for her aunt's rheumatism.

"Of course we write in English," snapped Mrs Kelly, "what do you think?"

"If Our Lady knows what's in our hearts," said Sister Mahony, "why does she need to have it on a postcard?"

"Ah. An interesting point," said Mr Thomson. He started to talk about recent apparitions of Our Lady and how petitions had been presented to her, apparently with her favour, in such a way. It was a subject close to his heart and he might have talked for hours, had not Mrs Kelly interrupted, anxious that the limelight be refocused on Anne Marie. "Excuse me, Mr Thomson, it's nearly time. Now I shall go first in the procession with Anne Marie and Mr Painscastle, if you'll be so kind. No hymns please just at the beginning, if you don't mind, though we can all sing the Lourdes hymn later. Anne Marie gets a bit nervous, you see, and then there are these silly boys who . . . ah! Here she comes now."

On cue, Anne Marie appeared in the doorway. She wore her school uniform, and her hair, covered by her mother's mantilla, was neatly brushed. There was no expression on her face at all.

"Well now, Anne Marie," said her mother gently, "are you ready?"

"Yes, Mum," said Anne Marie without a trace of the fidgety nerves she had displayed for Reverend Mother.

"Very well then. Shall we be off?"

"Rarin' to go!" said Mrs Evans-Blow with a heartiness that rang false in the porcelain-fine atmosphere. Kevin looked up with a nasty grin on his face. "Say a prayer for me, pig-face," and Anne Marie came out of her trance-like state just long enough to say, "Shut up you!"

It was twenty past six. Would Our Lady be punctual? They left the Kelly house and trooped up the path. Mr Blackaby shut the gate carefully behind them. Curtains tweaked, home-goers stopped and stared curiously.

Anne Marie walked rather fast. Her mother trotted by her side. Nobody spoke.

There was a cloud over the moon tonight and Mr Painscastle looked up anxiously at the sky. Maybe it would rain. But the air was soft, voluptuous almost, with a fine fast wind that skittered through the trees and pulled the clouds along. "Turning a bit chilly," said Miss Finch, though in fact it was not. Her heart was pounding busily.

At the end of the road, Anne Marie turned left and went down the hill. These were large detached houses, plump and sleek behind laurel hedges and curving gravel paths. Lights twinkled behind leaded windows and large silvery cars were poised like panthers. Behind one such window, Rachel Gold struggled with an essay on Bismarck and dreamed of love.

The common, unfenced, bordered the other side of this road. Anne Marie walked until she found a place where a path ran between hawthorn bushes and turned into it.

They passed no one except a man walking his dog and a late jogger. "Whoops!" said Mrs Evans-Blow as she nearly tripped over a hummock in the darkness.

"Mind how you go," said Mr Blackaby.

Anne Marie wove her way through the bushes. There was no logic to the path she took except that it was the one she had always followed before. The hawthorns grew thickly and then sparse. Now they curved in a sickle shape around an arena of empty grass, a space cut off from the rest of the common. She walked to the centre and stopped, before a hawthorn that seemed no different from any other hawthorn. Miss Finch gasped. Angelina crossed herself.

Now having stopped, Anne Marie turned and raised her hands as if uncertain. Mrs Kelly took over. "Right, everybody. Stand back if you please. Mrs Markinowski, could you stand back a bit?"

"I have a torch," said Mr Thomson. "Would it be permitted?"

"I should have thought candles . . ." said Sister Mahony.

Angelina suddenly began to sing in a quavery falsetto that made everybody jump, "Hail Queen of Heav'n, the Ocean

Star . . ." "Ssh," said Mrs Evans-Blow a little crossly. "Perhaps later," added Mr Blackaby more kindly. "I'm sorry," said Angelina humbly, "I sing later."

"Shall we all sing later?" said Sister Mahony.

"Perhaps Mr Painscastle would lead us in the rosary."

"I think perhaps we should all be quiet," said Mr Blackaby. They had fanned round in a semi-circle. Anne Marie, apparently dazed, stood in the middle.

"Excuse me, how do we know when anything's happening?" said Mrs Markinowski in a loud whisper.

"Hush," said Mr Painscastle. "I think you'll *know*," he added.

"Were you here when she came last time?" persisted Mrs Markinowski. Linda Markinowski fidgeted and giggled, turning to look at the gang of boys in the distance. That one with the earring was quite good-looking.

And suddenly those watching were aware that Anne Marie went rigid as though an electric current had passed through her body. Without a word, she dropped to her knees on the cold damp ground.

"She's here!" hissed Sister Mahony. But nobody except Linda Markinowski needed to be told that.

"Did you see those leaves?" whispered Mrs Evans-Blow. "A shiver ran through those leaves! I'm sure of it!"

"Hush," said Mr Painscastle.

"Hush," said Mrs Kelly.

Anne Marie remained kneeling, arms held down by her sides, hands turned to the front. Her face in the shaky light of Mr Thomson's torch held a strange expression, an unblinking smile, her head on one side. She did not look herself at all. Without speaking, the onlookers began to creep forward until they had almost surrounded her. When Mr Blackaby waved a hand in front of her face, she did not react. Then they began to hear a one-sided conversation:

"*Yes, I am.*
Yes, they did.
No, they don't.

Oh yes, I do."

Linda Markinowski slunk off. The boys lingered uneasily thirty yards away.

"What is it, then," said one, "bleedin' lunatics?"

"Huh!" said Linda. "She says she's having a bleedin' vision, don't she?"

"What? *Nah?*"

"Yeah. Dumb, isn't it?"

"What, she thinks she's seeing a bleeding vision?"

"Yeah."

"S'truth!"

"Yeah."

"I can't see no bleedin' vision."

'Well, of *course* you can't."

"What are they, some sort of nutters?"

"Nah," said Linda, "they're Catholics, aren't they?"

"'Ere," said the leader, "Bonko's a Catholic, aren't you?"

"Norrany more," said Bonko.

"What bleedin' vision does she think she's seeing then?"

"Oh, I don't know, Virgin Mary or something."

"Fuckin' hell!" said the leader, momentarily almost impressed. "Fuckin' hell!"

"Yeah," said Linda.

"Here, Bonko, she says that girl's seeing the Virgin Mary!"

"I heard," said Bonko.

"What shall we do? Give 'em a fright? Here," said the leader, suddenly convulsed with laughter, "I'll show 'em something. Shall I show 'em? Shall I give 'em a bleedin' vision?"

"You can get ten years for that," said Linda. She giggled.

"What's your name, then?"

"Linda."

"Hi, Linda. Hey lads this is Linda. I'm Dave."

"Hi, Dave."

"'N this is Bonko. We call him that 'cause he's bonko, aren't you Bonko? 'N this is Tish. 'N this is Briggsy."

"Hi."

"Oi, you lot," Dave called out. "Wanna see something then?"

None of those standing behind Anne Marie appeared to take any notice.

"Less go," grumbled Tish, "this is boring."

"Yeah," said Bonko. "Shut up Dave, willya?"

"Wasting our bleedin' time, aren't we?" said Dave. "C'mon then. Coming, Linda?"

"Nah," said Linda. "I've got to stay with my mum, haven't I?"

"See you then."

Meanwhile Anne Marie still knelt in her trance. Mr Thomson's torch shone full into her face but she seemed quite unaware of it. After a while, she said, "Yes, I see, you want people to honour your name." Then she nodded and smiled a little more, her eyes still fixed. It looked as if a wooden puppet performed all these motions.

"The cards! Tell her to show Our Lady the cards!" whispered Miss Finch.

"She can't hear you," said Mr Thomson.

"Ought we to start singing now?" wondered Mrs Evans-Blow.

"Would Mr Painscastle perhaps like to lead us in the Rosary?" said Mrs Kelly, turning round. Her eyes had an ecstatic gleam.

Anne Marie went on nodding and smiling for a few minutes longer and then she held out the cards in a sheaf. "I've got these for you. Is this all right? Can you see them?"

"What a way to talk to Our Blessed Lady," said Sister Mahony.

"I'm sorry, but it's my belief you're being made fools of," said Mrs Markinowski. "I don't think . . ."

"Be quiet!" hissed Mr Painscastle.

"When will you come back?" said Anne Marie. "What do you want me to do?"

"Is she going away?" said Miss Finch.

"I think she going now," said Angelina dolefully. "Oh, look. She gone."

Anne Marie had suddenly come out of her trance. She rose awkwardly to her feet and turned round blinking. "Why's he got that light in my eyes?" she demanded.

"Are you all right?" asked her mother.

"Yes, Mum."

"Has she gone now? Will she come back?"

Anne Marie shrugged. Linda Markinowski could be heard sniffing loudly.

"Is all right I sing now?" asked Angelina.

"Did she see my card?" asked Miss Finch. "What did she say?"

"Just a minute. . . .' said Mr Blackaby. "Don't crowd her now."

"I did see something going through the trees," said Mrs Evans-Blow.

"Is that all? Can we go now?" said Mrs Markinowski.

"As though someone stood there," said Mrs Evans-Blow. "A weight bowing the branches down."

Miss Finch sighed, sadly. "I didn't see anything," she said. "Nothing at all."

"Naughty, naughty," said Milly the next morning. "You're late."

"I overslept," said Rachel.

"There were great excitements at prayers," said Joanna. "Everybody fainted. First Karen O'Rourke in the first year and then three other kids. Thump! It was like dominoes."

"It's all that Kelly girl's fault. She's got the juniors all worked up. Apparently Our Lady made another appearance on the common last night. I think that's why. Suddenly everyone went hysterical."

"Was Kelly there this morning?"

"No, she didn't come in. I think that was part of the trouble. Everyone was telling all sorts of stories. It was most peculiar."

"And Reverend Mother gave us one of her special little talks about how some *vulgar common gels* were spreading wicked rumours and it was the duty of the rest of us to ignore these *vulgar common gels* under pain of hell."

"You know," said Joanna, "the thing she can't stand is that it's a vulgar common gel who's having these visions. Now if it was someone classy like our Rachel, it would be different."

"I'm afraid I can't help you there," said Rachel. "Jews don't have visions."

"Couldn't you try?" said Milly. "Just a teeny one?"

"I'm sorry," said Rachel with surprisingly more vehemence than the subject seemed to demand, "I'm not that sort of person. I'm not going to have a vision."

Chapter 7

"Who on earth does she think she is?" demanded Sister Mark. "This morning I had to go to the medical cupboard to get — sorry, Sister Aloysius — some Tampax, and she accused me of using too many. Too many! What can she mean? Either you bleed or you don't."

"We never used to talk of such things," said Sister Aloysius sadly, "and you know, I really can't see that we're the better for it now."

"Well, I think we are," said Sister Mark firmly. "And quite frankly, I'm glad that we don't have to stagger around in woollen knickers any more. Or kiss the floor and scourge ourselves. But Sister Scholastica, I think, still wishes that we did."

"Sister Scholastica is a good nun," said Sister Aloysius. The other nuns fell into a glum silence as they confronted this blank wall of a statement.

If Sister Scholastica guessed that they discussed her so, she gave no signs of it, as she glided swiftly and silently through the corridors, unsmiling except when sarcasm briefly twitched her lips, her eyes never straying, her voice never raised. A good nun submerges herself entirely in the love of God. She is a vessel, merely, for a greater force. She must take as her model Mary, the passive, the stoical, the almost unmentioned. A good nun must barely exist.

Of course, a good nun does not come into the world fully fledged as such. The calm, obedient exterior conceals many a mighty struggle. Sister Scholastica had once been somebody else, a girl called Clare.

In childhood, Clare had been chiefly noted for her strong will and the loudness of her voice. But at adolescence a heavy curtain seemed to fall between herself and the rest of the world. She watched the other girls in her class as they giggled, gossiped, talked of bosoms, and love bites and periods. The classroom crackled with whiffs of the adult world like some dangerous, volatile gas. Clare was frightened and hid in the little chapel, with its cool marble smell and blue ceiling painted with golden stars. And gradually, as the other girls showed off their talents for hockey, parading in school plays, swimming, or simply making boys fall in love with them, Clare found something she was good at. She was good at religion.

She went devotedly to church, kept the First Fridays, and whispered many rosaries. She became a Child of Mary, and went on retreats. She threw herself into these things with enthusiasm. Sometimes the fear overwhelmed her still and she lay in bed at night hugging her pale thin body and weeping. But it was freedom that she found oppressive, not confinement. She longed for the embrace of a rule so severe that she would grow against it like a cordon apple tree. At seventeen, she said goodbye to the dangerous world, and entered the novitiate. Her parents, a quiet, elderly doctor and his wife, were horrified, but powerless against the force of their daughter's will. She did not scream or shout now, but compressed her lips and went white. They let her go, and within three years both were dead.

At last, behind the high walls, she found peace. While the other novices fretted and pined at the loss of freedom, she prospered. The older nuns recognised in her unwavering devotion a creature of rare qualities. Once, as a test, the novice mistress told her to cut the grass outside the convent front door — with a pair of nail scissors. This could be seen from the road by casual passers-by — the humiliation was both public and private. Another novice so tested had collapsed in hysterics after a few hours and left the convent the next day. But she persevered, while people looking through the gates giggled, until finally at dusk she was released; stiff, damp and sore-fingered, but apparently impassive.

But now the ruthless certainties of the old rule were gone, and she found herself thrown back on those old enemies, reason and common sense. In addition, she found after all her years of submission to God and the rule, a certain amount of discontent was creeping into her soul. Discontent with what? With the order? No, she still wanted no other life for herself. With God? But that was too huge and horrifying a thought. What was it then? Perhaps it was a feeling that after year upon year of struggle at her chosen profession, by now there should be something to show for it. After all, the great athlete looks for the gold medal, the scientist wins the Nobel prize, the actor receives his Oscar. These rewards were their due for effort and dedication. She too had a right to expect the supreme reward when the soul is swept away by the Love of God, everything lost in blinding joy. Yet God's demands on her seemed unremitting, and His rewards further away than ever. What was to be done? She behaved in the only way she knew, by making things harder and harder for herself and for those around her. But the despair was there still; it would not go away.

Taking IIIa for Religious Studies was a greater penance than ever since that little minx Anne Marie had started telling her tales. Now there was a continual mood of restlessness in the class, a subterranean excitement, especially today when Anne Marie, whose attendance had been intermittent recently, was present. They could take Sister's word for nothing, they needed always to be asking questions, criticising, demanding. Anne Marie Kelly sat near the back, not working, not even as far as one could tell, daydreaming, simply occupying the space of her plump body. It seemed hardly enough to fill out a life, and yet . . . Sister could not help feeling as she looked at her something uncomfortably akin to the feelings of a scorned woman as she confronts her rival in love. The more that Sister thought about it, the more she was inclined to believe that Anne Marie, stupid, young and undeserving, had known that supreme spiritual experience, the experience which had been denied to her. The outsider had beaten the champion; the Nobel prize had been won by the assistant and not the scientist.

SEEING THINGS

Today she dictated notes. One was not supposed to dictate notes but with a class like IIIa what else was there to do? Never in a thousand years could their own thought processes take them where Sister wanted them taken. "A sacrament is defined by both the outward sign and the inward grace which follows. Both these things must be present. In the sacrament of Confession. . ."

Rosemary Welch interrupted without putting up her hand. "But Sister, what I don't understand is . . ."

Sister gave her a glance that would quell a forest fire. "*Yes*, Rosemary?"

"I don't understand why you have to confess sins to the priest. Why can't I just confess them to you. . . ." (A snigger ran round the class. Sister glared) ". . . or to my mother, or the police or someone?"

"Because, as you would know very well if you had been listening to one half of the things I told you, neither I, nor your mother, or indeed the police . . ." she paused in her turn to extract a half-hearted giggle from the class ". . . have the power given by God to forgive sins. Only a priest, and Jesus Christ himself, can do this. If you don't know that by now then I wonder what sort of a Catholic you can be."

"But, Sister," said another girl, "supposing somebody bad, someone who'd just murdered someone went to confession, wouldn't the priest have to go to the police and tell them?"

"No, child, he would not have to."

"But wouldn't it be against the law?"

"We are talking about God's Law, and that, in the end, is the only Law that counts. What a priest hears in confession, no matter how terrible, is a secret he must never reveal. He must go to the grave before he reveals it. Now, can we please get on with our notes? Sit up, please, Carol Ryder."

"But, Sister," began someone else.

Sister picked up her notes and tried to carry on where she had left off. "In the sacrament of Confession, the power to hear and forgive sins has been vested in the priest by the words of Our Lord. . . ."

Sister Mark said to her at lunch, "Sister, you aren't eating a thing. You'll make yourself ill. Have some more; have an apple at least."

Sister Scholastica felt a stab of panic. Controlling herself, she said, "Sister, I am quite capable of looking after my own health, thank you. You might do better to attend to your own business. There is a button on your cardigan that will fall off shortly if you don't see to it."

After lunch the panic was still there. She went into the chapel to say a few prayers before afternoon classes began but she could not concentrate on the words. On the way out, she almost bumped into Rachel, who was as usual rushing up the stairs far too fast. She had to put out her hand to steady her, touching Rachel's thin shoulder.

"Sorry, Sister," said Rachel with a grin.

Sister tried to smile back. She intended to say something kind, but what came out only wiped the smile off Rachel's face. "Rachel Gold," she said. "I might have known it. Everywhere I look, there's Rachel Gold causing trouble!"

Chapter 8

"Oh, it's you, Father Joyce," said Mrs Mangan, without enthusiasm. "You'd better come in."

The front parlour was intricate and highly polished. A variety of gilt and crystalline surfaces reflected a hectic glitter. Photographs of grandchildren were massed like votive objects.

"How is Mr Mangan?" he asked.

"Wheezing like an old bellows as usual. He's not long for us if you ask me, Father. I suppose you want a cup of tea."

"Don't let me put you to any trouble."

"Trouble? When have I ever been afraid of trouble, you tell me that? Now, have you been to Social Services again for me, Father?"

"Yes, I did, but I'm afraid I couldn't get anything new. They say your allowance went up six months ago and they can't increase it again."

"Oh did they? Did they say that? Well, listen, Father, just you get on to them again and tell them can they stop the shops putting their prices up? Because if they can do that they can leave their old allowance alone but they can't, can they? Do you know the price of nappy cream has gone up twice in the last year? And his knickers. Do you know how many pairs of knickers he gets through in a year?"

"Why not phone them yourself? You could explain all that much better than I can."

"So you're giving up on me are you, Father? You don't want to be bothered any more. Well, if that's how you feel. . . ."

"But if you were to tell them yourself it might. . . . No, no, I'll phone again."

Mrs Mangan nodded. "You do that, Father. Now then, I expect you'd like to see how we are this morning."

"Ah . . . yes."

"Look at the big smile we had for nurse this morning. Ah, she says, you are a happy boy this morning. Such a big smile. Yes, Father, you can come and pay us a little visit. We'd like that, we would."

Michael, her grandson, was in the back room. It had been decorated with animal wallpaper and mobiles hung over the bed. On one wall were certificates of attendance at Lourdes, on another some birthday cards had been pinned. It was spotlessly clean with a faint sweet smell of powder and antiseptic. In his huge cot, Michael's naked legs stirred beneath the padding of nappies and his curled hands clenched and unclenched. When his grandmother entered the room his eyes seemed to make a convulsive movement, focus momentarily and then his gaze drifted laxly around the room. His white skin was peppered with open sores. Only his grandmother's devotion had kept him alive so long, everybody said. He was fifteen years old.

She gazed down proudly and lovingly at him. "There now Michael. What about a big smile for the Father now?"

Mrs Glass met him more eagerly, opening the door before he had knocked, pulling him inside smiling. Bright pink lipstick smeared her teeth and her hair was a lemon yellow frizz. He tried not to register distaste at the smell of the house. "I'm so glad you came, Father. I've been wanting a word. Come in, come in."

"What can I do for you, Mrs Glass?"

She stopped in her tracks and turned. For a moment her eyes glowed like light bulbs and the crack of her smile widened. But as she talked her gaze swivelled everywhere. "Oh no, Father, you've got it wrong. It's not what you can do for me, it's what I can do for you. Sit down, sit down. Would you like some tea?"

Mrs Glass's little kitchenette was at the far end of her bedsit. She did not appear to have done any washing-up for several weeks now. He watched as she mixed tea bags, milk, sugar, salt and a good shaking of pepper in a mug. "It's the children, you see, Father, I have so much to give them, so much I want to share. I've told you about my gentleman friend, haven't I, Father? He wants to marry me you know, but don't tell anyone yet it's a secret, he said only the other day, why don't you ask the Father, and tell him you want a Sunday School class. You see with all my knowledge, all my experience, I can give them so much. . . ."

Miss Porret, a retired teacher, did not smile as she opened the door. "Doing your saintly duties again, Father? Visiting the sick and comforting the comfortless? Well, you'd better come in, though if you can get a smile out of her today, you're a better man than I am, Gunga Din. Do you know what I caught her doing today? Why she was only putting on her coat over her nightie and bedroom slippers, if you please. Told me she had to go to the chemist's to be weighed before lunch; got quite shirty when I said she had to go back to bed. Oh, she's really been reaching the heights today, I can tell you. Yesterday it was cutting little holes in the curtains to let the air in. God only knows what it'll be tomorrow. I suppose you've come cadging a cup of tea as usual, Father. Why don't you have a go at cheering her up while I put the kettle on. Might as well work for your living, eh, Father?"

It was nearly lunchtime when he reached Mrs Kelly's house. A faint smell of beefburgers came from within. There were no flowers or shrubs in the front garden and a broken bicycle lay in the long grass. But the paintwork was clean and the path had been swept. A Kelly child — Dermot was it? — opened the door and stood gazing up at him snottily.

"Mum!" he called out. "It's the priest."

"Oh it is, is it?" said Mrs Kelly's voice from within. "Well, ask him in." The child showed him into the clean, bare living room where another Kelly child — Steven? — was watching a schools programme about statistics. Mrs Kelly appeared, wiping her hands on her apron. "Boys, go and get your dinners in the kitchen." She clapped her hands and they disappeared like magicians' rabbits.

"Well, Father?" Mrs Kelly, to his relief, did not offer him tea.

"We can see the relevance of this approach," said the voice on the screen, "if we turn once more to our figures on migration."

"Just wanted to find out how you were all getting along, Mrs Kelly."

"Oh no, you did not. You did no such thing. You thought you could come here behind my Anne Marie's back and get me to say all sorts of nonsense."

"Here we see," went on the voice, "how the figures appear to rise sharply in the second half of 1975. But when we consider more closely we see . . ."

"Mrs Kelly, you and Anne Marie are my parishioners. I'd be failing in my duty if I didn't take an interest."

"Ah, but you don't want to take an interest do you? You're like all the others. You simply want to tell me that my girl's having hallucyations, don't you?"

But even her mispronunciation could not give Father Joyce the sense of moral superiority he felt he ought to have at this point. "No, Mrs Kelly, I don't think they're necessarily . . ." He strove vainly for a way of avoiding the word lest Mrs Kelly think he was trying to correct her.

"Well, let me show you this, Father." She took a letter from behind the clock. "'I can honestly say that until you sent the rosary which Our Lady had consented to bless, I had not been without pain for several years. But now my pain is gone and I am getting a good night's sleep. . . .' There! All the way from Solihull, that one. And here's one from Devon. 'Since receiving the medal blessed by Our Lady I have been most fortunate, last week I won fifty pounds on the Pools, and also a holiday for two in the Canaries run by *Woman's Own* magazine. . . .' There, Father. And I could show you a dozen more like that."

"This approach is essential," the disembodied voice said, "if we are not to allow irrelevancies and artificialities to cloud the true patterns as revealed by the figures themselves . . ."

"Mrs Kelly, all sorts of people claim to see Our Lady. We, the Church, have to be very careful before we can let other people believe . . ."

"Have you been to the common when she comes? No, of course you haven't. Well, let me tell you, all sorts of people go doubting and come back believing. If you saw Anne Marie there, you couldn't help believing. Four times she's come now, Our Blessed Lady has, and she'll come again. You see, Father, she has a special message for the world, and she's not going to stop coming until she's told Anne Marie that special message. . . ."

Dolly Masters was at the railings when Mr Painscastle arrived. Dolly, a voluminous woman, healthy pink cheeks hidden beneath an avalanche of clinging face powder, gave the impression of something seen through a magnifying mirror. Dolly specialised in weeping children and sad-eyed dogs. Last summer, she'd tried a new version of the weeping child; this one had his trousers down round his ankles and was looking soulfully over his shoulder. It had sold as quickly as she could turn out copies. "I call it my Botty period, darlings," she had said loudly over a cup of tea and a bacon sandwich at Jim's stall. "One for the pervs. Still never mind, eh? It paid for me holiday in Ibiza, didn't it?"

Mr Painscastle came up and was looking intently at a landscape. Dolly knew Mr Painscastle might be persuaded to buy an occasional picture, though what he had really come for was a serious talk about Art. "Hallo, darling," said Dolly, like an old hooker ("which is just what I am, darlings, a whore of the art world"), "how's life treating you today then?"

Mr Painscastle considered before replying. "Not so bad. I can't complain." He regretted Dolly's lapse into vulgarity and hoped she would return to a safer world of sunsets and tears. "And you? Business going well, I hope?"

"Bloody terrible," said Dolly cheerfully.

"Not the best time of year, perhaps?"

"There's no best time, darling. It's all bloody terrible. Isn't it, Rose? All bloody terrible."

"You're telling me," said Rose sadly. Rose was seagulls in the mist and clippers in the wind.

"Still one day the Pools'll come up. Live in hopes, that's it."

"Someday my prince will come," said Rose. "Oh my Gawd, Doll, look who it isn't."

"Blimey, Honest Ron and his squeaking doggies. Here we go, girls, hang on to your knickers."

"I don't see Miss Carmichael today. Isn't this normally her . . ."

"Carmen? Oh lord, haven't you heard? Oh yes, Sir, every one an original. Dollars? I don't mind dollars. Not yen though, I'm afraid. Sorry." Two anxious Japanese tourists who seemed not to be enjoying themselves had stopped to look. "Genuine works of art — a real investment."

"Has anything happened to Miss Carmichael?" Mr Painscastle went on. "I ask because you see . . ."

"What? Oh yes, oils, none of your acrylic rubbish. I said none of your ac- Never mind. Yes, oils."

"And this is Engrish Traditioner?" enquired the Japanese.

"Oh, it's English Traditional all right. You wouldn't find anything more English Traditional than one of my paintings."

"That's right," said the man with the suitcase and sharp raincoat. "As English as matzo balls and my uncle Morrie's nose, eh, Dolly?"

"Oh, hallo Ron," said Dolly, without enthusiasm. "You here again then?"

"I most certainly am. And while I'm here perhaps the gentleman would like to take a shufty at these novelties. Friendly Fido, wags his head, look. Does everything a real doggie does except whoopsie on the carpet."

The Japanese examined them with more interest than they had shown in the paintings. Dolly pulled a face behind their backs.

"Miss Carmichael . . ." persisted Mr Painscastle.

"Bastard," mouthed Dolly. "Flash bastard. Ooh."

"I wondered . . ."

"God, he's not buying a bloody Fido, is he?" exclaimed Dolly. "He bloody is. He's buying a bloody Fido. Well, of all the . . . I've had enough. I'm off for a cuppa. Keep an eye on me masterpieces, won't you, Rose?"

"I always keep my eye on your masterpieces, Dol," said Ron, winking with glee over his sale. "Don't I?"

"And you can shut up," said Dolly. She went off.

"Do *you* know anything about Miss Carmichael?" said Mr Painscastle to Ron.

"Miss who? Oh *Carmen*. You mean old Carmen." Ron burst into song. "*Torry*-ador, oh Torryador . . ."

"Shut up, Ron," said Rose. "Carmen's ill, dear, didn't you know?"

"No, indeed I didn't. Nothing serious, I hope."

Rose pursed her lips and stared ahead of her.

"Nothing serious, I hope," said Ron, "as the laughing hyena said to the elephant."

"Miss Carmichael and I are almost neighbours," said Mr Painscastle. "I do hope there's nothing seriously wrong."

Rose laughed without humour. "Wrong? I'm afraid it's the big C, darling."

Ron paused from winding a key in a furry backside. "Oh dear. Poor old Carmen. Poor old girl."

"I bet . . ."

"Cancer," said Rose shortly. "The doctors reckon it's incurable. They give her six months."

Chapter 9

Saint Peter sat enthroned with a plastic bag over his head. Incense rose in a cloud and a woman's voice sang the Kyrie in tones of piercing sweetness. "*Per omnia saecula saeculorum,*" intoned the priest, and the words had lost none of their shuddering power for Hugo. Here in the Oratory it was not difficult to believe in God. *Per omnia saecula saeculorum*! The ages unrolled like a great carpet and somewhere at the end of it sat God enthroned in glittering majesty.

It was a pity about the plastic bag. Along with the scaffolding and a smell of plaster dust mingling with the incense it belonged to the renovations that had been going on for some weeks; but it could not alter that central fact: God was here, as he was in any of His churches.

As He was in any of His churches — and here of course was the problem. As He was in some appalling plastic and concrete aircraft hangar in Muswell Hill or Tooting Bec? As He was in that travesty that had replaced the dignity of the old Latin Mass? As He was in some suburban eyesore where — horror of horrors — the congregation turned to each other and shook hands and kissed cheeks in the middle of the service? God did not stand up well to democracy, thought Hugo — and yet, God was God and Faith was Faith. Or were they? How long could both survive in Tooting Bec?

A bell tinkled, although the smartly dressed congregation knelt already in profound silence and the miracle of transformation began. *Hoc est enim corpus meum* . . . The miracle, cataclysmic and yet commonplace was at this moment being performed all over London, all over Europe, astonishingly multiplied.

Of course, it was this mix of miraculous and commonplace that was one of the charms of the Catholic Church; the faithful were right to expect a little encouragement from on high as they groped their way thanklessly through life. Just a glimpse between the clouds would be enough for most people. It would be enough for himself, he thought; how his faith would be revitalised if he could catch just a little chink of light. But so far, he had not found it. Or had found only darkness. The Virgin of Bernadette and the Fatima children had ranted and raved like a fishwife; if she really brought God's word with her, then it was too horrible to contemplate. Only a child could expect everything about faith to be easy and acceptable, but he could not help regretting those old days and the wonderful stories which fed his imagination just as the stories of Jason and Odysseus had done. Now they had all gone: Saint Patrick was really a Welshman; Saint Sebastian did not die from arrow wounds; Saint Cecilia knew nothing at all about music; Saint Catherine did not die on the wheel; Saint Francis of Assisi was really called Giovanni; Wenceslas, who had not been a king anyway, stayed home when it snowed; and as for Saint Christopher, the most romantic of all, he was so phony that the Pope had tried to demote him entirely, and it was only after the pleading of Italian film stars frightened of their own driving that he had been reluctantly reinstated.

That left God. And God was harder than ever to find these days. Some people said God was gay, some said He was a woman, or a bad case of mushroom poisoning. Worse than that, most people simply did not care one way or the other. God was outmoded, like the military twostep. When Hugo left the Oratory at the end of Mass and decided to cycle through the park, he was nearly beaten back by a huge sea of joggers, sweating, panting, purple-faced. Vans and television crews followed the great surge with interest, and banners proclaimed in great letters the name of the Sunday paper which was sponsoring the whole parade. People were collapsing, even dying. This was today's God; Jehovah had been replaced by Narcissus, and his exhausted flagellants urged themselves on even unto death in his gruelling service.

When he got home, Hugo spread his notes out on the table and tried to concentrate on his work. But something odd was happening. Lines from the popular paperback he was determined not to write kept weaving themselves into his prose: 'It was a chill February evening, when Bernadette Soubirous, an asthmatic child of thirteen from one of the poorest families in the village, decided to go out to gather wood. . . .' Across his desk he seemed to see the pained and indignant countenances of Saint Teresa, Dame Julian, Richard Rolle and Saint John of the Cross. 'We had thought better of you,' they seemed to say reprovingly. But what was it to them? *They* were never faced with problems like eviction threats. What would Dame Julian in her cell have done if her landlord had confronted her with a letter such as the one Hugo had received only the other day?

He carried on writing for a while, and then sat back to see what his pen had produced: '*Aquero*, Bernadette had called it, as she knelt by the icy river to take off her clogs, *aquero* which was simply the local dialect word for "that thing", a white shape that might or might not have been a girl. But the next time she saw *that thing* she recognised the beautiful Lady. . . .' You could almost hear the lush violins and see Jennifer Jones tripping through the mists. Well, never mind. Bills must be paid, and what people wanted these days were signs and wonders. Then he remembered Antonia and her South London schoolgirl. There was Mr Gold's Italian housekeeper apparently agog to tell the tale. Pulling a face at Dame Julian, he reached for a sheet of notepaper, and began, 'Dear Mr Gold. . . .'

Nevertheless, it came as something of a surprise a few days later when Mr Gold actually replied. By all means let him come and interview Angelina. The only trouble was that he and his wife would be away on a conference over the next few weeks, but he was quite sure that his daughter would be delighted to look after Hugo and introduce him to Angelina. At this point panic set in. A trip to the wilds of South London and some gawky teenager and a mad Italian at the end of it — a journey through suburban wastes on one of those alien buses with a huge number (nowhere nice, he thought, was served by a number higher than 137). Right up till the last minute he thought about excuses he could make not to go, but he went, in the end. The familiar 49 bus took him some of the way at least, across the river, through Battersea and then into South London. At last, he thought, I have come to it. Now I am the man on the Clapham omnibus.

Beyond Clapham, a kind conductor and the *A—Z* took him to the opulent road where the Golds lived by the side of the common. Their house was big and solid, mid-wars Tudor, embalmed behind dark indeterminate shrubs. A single hybrid tea rose of a peculiar shade of orange lingered on a spindly bush. It spoke, this house, of bills paid and dues not forgotten. It spoke of solidity, of sound commercial values, of respectability. Hugh shuddered.

He rang the doorbell and waited for the gawky teenager. Instead the door was opened by Rachel. "Oh," she said. "Oh, I thought you'd be . . ." Left in reluctant charge by her father, she had been expecting a fat middle-aged man. She was as startled as Hugo. She wore, since she had not anticipated Hugo being worth a change of clothes, her school uniform of blue skirt and white blouse. Her waist was so small he might have cupped it with his hands; above the virginal white of her blouse her hair made a glowing cloud. As she moved, taking coats and opening doors, her gestures were graceful as a dancer's. Though her voice, by contrast, was that of any schoolgirl with the flat nasal twang of her generation. "Can I get you a drink?" He accepted the drink, a sherry, though he loathed sherry. The living room was just as he imagined it: full of dull, overblown furniture. He sank down in a sofa so big it might have come from an ocean liner. In fact it could even have taken to the seas itself, a huge smooth streamlined hulk, covered in cream silk.

The girl seemed at a loss. "This is a bit awful," she said. "I don't know what to say." He thought she was trying to tell him some unpleasant fact about himself, and already awry from unfamiliar sensation, it took him some time to realise that she was talking about Angelina, who was not there. Mr Gold had taken for granted her willingness to be interviewed, but she had reacted with sudden indignation only that morning. "I don't care about no man writing no book. Today afternoon I go see the man with my feet. If I'm back, okay. If I not back, then is his bad luck, I'm sorry." She was not back. Rachel felt she was making some kind of a point, but it was hard to see what.

"I'm sorry," repeated Rachel, "I don't know what to say. I didn't have your number, or I'd have rung."

Sorrow became her, thought Hugo. "It really doesn't matter. This is — er — very good sherry."

"We keep it for visitors," said Rachel with the transparency of youth. She blinked. "Have you come a long way?"

Yes, oh yes. How could she know how far? "No, not really. Only Chelsea."

"Chelsea," she breathed, as though he had said the Promised Land. "Chelsea!"

He smiled back at her, a slightly patronising smile. He felt that he could be patronising in South London. "Chelsea's very nice. But I shall have to move out soon. My lease is running out."

"Oh dear," she said softly, as though he had told her of some great personal tragedy. Which of course he had. "Where will you go?"

"Who knows? Somewhere round here, perhaps."

"Oh that would be nice!" she exclaimed, and then fell silent as though she had said too much.

"Yes, wouldn't it?" he said at his most avuncular. "You have this lovely common to look at."

"Do you like it?" she said. "It's full of dog muck and crisp packets, and — oh, dirty old men and . . ." Again panic seemed to seize her and she fell silent like a trapped bird.

"And the Virgin Mary?" he questioned gently.

They smiled at each other in sudden guilty complicity. Hugo began to feel relaxed. "Yes," she said. "Oh dear, yes."

"Or so your Arabella thinks."

"Angelina."

"Angelina. But she won't tell me about it."

"I can't think why. She's been boring the pants off — sorry — she's been boring everybody else to death with it. Our Lady and Anne Marie Kelly. Personally I think the child's off her head. We all do."

"Do you know this Anne Marie Kelly then?"

"Oh yes. We go to the same school. I thought you knew."

"I know almost nothing. Isn't she at a Catholic school?"

"Yes, the Seven Sorrows convent. It's where I go, too."

"But you're — pardon me — Jewish."

"Yes, it's silly really, isn't it? Mummy thinks convents turn out nice, well-behaved girls. And — you know how it is — she doesn't believe in too much Jewishness. She thinks it's repressive."

"Repression doesn't come worse than Catholics sometimes."

"I know; you don't have to tell me. When I started at the school, one little old nun took me aside and whispered, 'Now dear, you may find some people here who won't be very nice to you, because after all, it was the Jews who killed Our Lord, wasn't it? But as long as you don't do anything to single yourself out I don't suppose anyone will be too unkind.'"

"Good heavens! Did you tell your mother that?"

"No. I was only eleven, and at that age you can't really sort out when things are wrong, can you? I thought it was just her way of being kind to me."

"So how did you manage not to single yourself out?"

"I tried to behave like a good Catholic girl. I went to prayers, I went to Mass, I did everything except go to Communion. And I became the star pupil in Religious Knowledge lessons. I still go to those. I quite enjoy them actually. It's relaxing in a funny sort of way, because it doesn't matter, not like the things I'm doing at A-level, I mean. It's not so good this year because we have this dreadful nun who's always on at me; I think she hates me for some reason. But I still enjoy it; trying to follow the logic and putting two and two together to make six. Oh God, I forgot; you're a Catholic too, aren't you, Daddy said. I hope you don't think I'm being rude."

"Not at all. It's rather refreshing."

"I mean, it's not that I don't believe in God. I do, at least I sort of do, though he doesn't look anything like God in the pictures."

"I think everybody has to make their own selection of things to believe, don't you? After all, in the end it's a very personal thing. Sometimes I'm a rather odd sort of Catholic myself. I do some very un-Catholic things." He thought of Antonia.

"Of course, you're a writer, aren't you?" This fact which had not been in the least interesting to her when he had been a fat old man turned out to be fascinating when he proved to be a good-looking youngish one. "It's awful of me, but I'm afraid I haven't read any of your books. Does that sound terrible?"

"No, of course not," he said, but naturally it did. He thought, sadly, what use is it my being a writer if people like this lovely girl have never heard of me? "Do tell me," he said, trying to get the subject on to safer ground, "what do you know about Anne Marie? Is she happy at school, for example?"

"It's hard to tell. She doesn't look like the sort of girl who has any feelings about anything. The other girls tease her I think."

"They don't like her?"

"Not that exactly. But her hem hangs down and she sort of looks as though she smells even if she doesn't. I don't think she actually smells. And she wears that kind of cheap school uniform that goes all shiny. We're supposed to get it at Peter Jones. There are an awful lot of snobs at our school, I'm afraid."

"And Anne Marie isn't well off?"

"Her mother goes out cleaning. Sorry, I sound frightful. I'm not like that at all. Well, I suppose I am, we all are a bit. But everyone else, their fathers are accountants and bankers and things like that; and there's poor Anne Marie, who just doesn't fit. It's not her fault."

"Tell me everything you can about her."

There was not much to tell, though Rachel was intelligent and observant enough. She told him the facts, but it was never facts that were lacking, thought Hugo, in these stories. What was not there was the one definitive fact, the thing that might swing the balance one way or the other. He decided that he would try and get in touch with Anne Marie and her family. Antonia was right; this was all more interesting than it had first seemed. And this pretty young girl was interesting too, and for the next hour or so, he gave himself up to the pleasures of talking to her, quizzing her about her ambitions, perhaps even flirting a little. Meanwhile, Angelina did not return and he drank a second glass of sherry.

Chapter 10

In Reverend Mother's study, a battle was in progress. The Bishop had sent Monsignor Pole, his representative, to investigate the rumours. Monsignor Pole's approach was gentle but inexorable. "I do sympathise," he said. "These must be trying times," he said. And then pounced. "But what I can't help wondering, Reverend Mother, is whether you and your staff might not — quite unwittingly, of course — have brought some of this down on your own heads."

Reverend Mother stiffened. At present she resembled some great flightless bird which had backed itself into an impasse. "I don't quite know what you're implying, Monsignor, but . . ."

"Good heavens, Reverend Mother, I hope you don't imagine that the Bishop sent me here to try and trap you. But all events must have causes and we would be failing in our duty if we did not try to examine very meticulously what the causes of this one might be."

"I see," said Reverend Mother tightly. "And what conclusions have you come to?"

Monsignor laughed. "Oh, we're a long long way from conclusions yet. If indeed we ever reach them. This is more in the nature of . . . a putting out of preliminary feelers. Of the most tenuous unassertive sort. Of course, it may be that we will have to subject every aspect of the girl's story to rigorous examination. But that time is not with us yet."

"Well then, what do your preliminary feelers tell you?"

"The point is this. Might there not in the past months have been, shall we say, an unwise emphasis in doctrinal studies? A stress, however slight, however unintentional, towards the kind of outworn superstitions we are now trying so hard to clear away from the Church?"

"No," said Reverend Mother. "There might not."

"You seem very certain."

"At the Seven Sorrows," said Reverend Mother, "we regard Religious Studies as the most important subject on the syllabus. Do you imagine I would hand it over to just anybody? I examine the syllabus myself most carefully every year."

"I only wish some of our brethren could say as much. But Reverend Mother . . ."

"But, Monsignor?"

"What we teach now will shape the Church of the future. We must be ever vigilant."

"Yes, I know, but . . ."

"And you'd be surprised what things can lurk in the odd corners of a convent. Only the other day I came across an old nun teaching — still teaching — her class that to get rid of the devil all you had to do was to make the Sign of the Cross on his tail."

Reverend Mother allowed herself a faint smile. "I was taught that myself, many years ago."

"And I too. I too. But we owe future generations better than that, do we not, Reverend Mother? If we clutter their heads with superstitions how will we prevent more of our children being lost to atheism and ignorance?"

"But we don't clutter their heads!"

"Do you not?" he said with a charming smile. "Are you sure that among all your good intentions, some things aren't allowed to seep in? Some of the more unwise enthusiasms of female saints? Some of the more dubious transports of the ecstatics?"

"Dubious? Unwise?" said Reverend Mother faintly. "Are we talking about the Saints of God, Monsignor?"

"There are saints and saints," he went on pleasantly, "but not all saints are suitable as role models for adolescent girls, I think you'll agree."

"Are you suggesting that we shouldn't teach our girls to admire the saints?"

"If those saints are chosen carefully. Saint Thérèse of Lisieux for example shows how to be a saint without doing anything dangerous. But take Saint Bernadette. A young girl goes out for a walk in the cold and who does she meet but Our Blessed Lady? A wonderful story of humility and faith rewarded for you and I, Reverend Mother, for you and I. But tell such a story to a young impressionable girl, and what do you have?"

"What do you have, Monsignor?"

"Why, a Cinderella fantasy, with Our Lady playing the role of Prince Charming. Young girls are very vulnerable; we must not fill their heads with undesirable elements."

"Pardon me, Monsignor. I had no idea Saint Bernadette was an undesirable element."

"Now now, Reverend Mother, don't misunderstand me. I am talking about expediency."

"I understood we were talking about Our Blessed Lady."

"No, Reverend Mother at the moment we are not. We are talking about a young girl who appears to have had an hysterical experience. We are looking for what the causes of that experience might be."

"Then I suggest you go straightaway and talk to Anne Marie's mother. Now there's a hysterical experience for you. I really believe that woman is not in her right mind."

"If only we could."

"What do you mean?"

"Mrs Kelly flatly refuses to see us, or to let us interview Anne Marie."

"But that's disgraceful."

"It is indeed."

"Can you not apply pressure?"

He arched a delicate eyebrow. The rack, the wheel, the thumbscrew? "We shall, Reverend Mother. Believe me we shall apply pressure when the time is right."

"To refuse to see His Grace's representative!"

"Disgraceful indeed. But there again, Reverend Mother, I wonder if perhaps — quite inadvertently again, of course — you have not been playing into her hands."

"I really cannot see . . ."

Monsignor Pole sighed. Somewhere behind his breastbone indigestion was beginning to burn like the piercing tip of a sword. He thought of the lunch the good nuns had made him eat, flannelly roast chicken, overcooked vegetables, watery mash followed by apple pie of similar consistency all washed down by warm Spanish *Sauternes*. "I understand you have suspended Anne Marie Kelly from school."

"We had no choice. Her attendance has been erratic anyway since this miserable business started. She seems to believe she is a law unto herself. And when she comes it causes trouble."

"What kind of trouble?"

"Faintings, hysteria. All sorts of things. And then other girls who tease her and make a mockery of the thing. All most unfortunate."

"But by banning her, do you not encourage our enemies?"

"I don't see how."

"Come, come now! A convent school, suspending a girl for having seen Our Lady!"

"Or not having seen Our Lady."

"It's all a question of tactics. A question of subtlety."

"How do you suspend someone subtly?" asked Reverend Mother, on whom the strain was now beginning to show.

"If her presence is upsetting, then her absence must be even more so. You are giving the thing the chance to grow into a myth. At school every day the girls would soon grow bored with her and tease her out of it."

"Are you saying we should take her back?"

"I think you might find that difficult now. I imagine Mrs Kelly is making all the capital she can out of the affair. Didn't you read that piece in the local paper?"

"So what are we to do?"

"We can't turn back the clock. You can't unsuspend Anne Marie. For the moment then, do nothing. But I shall keep up my pressure on Mrs Kelly and in the end I have no doubt I shall be allowed to speak to young Anne Marie."

"And then?"

"Then I shall make my report to the Bishop and he will decide what steps to take next. It may be — and this is to be hoped — that the whole thing will die down with the minimum of intervention on our part. We may be able to subject Anne Marie to intensive physical and psychological tests to get to the root of all this...."

He sighed and delicately examined his fingers. They were long and pale with exquisitely shaped nails.

"Or, Monsignor?"

"Or we may be forced to the conclusion that Our Lady really has appeared to this little girl. And then, Reverend Mother, our troubles will really begin."

Another battle was taking place in Hugo's flat.

"Simple courtesy, darling, that's all it is."

"What on earth has courtesy to do with it?"

"Everything, I should have thought. Tom will bring June, Camilla will have Jamie and even Sarah can rustle up that chinless wonder of hers. Everyone except *me*. I'll have to turn up all on my own and everyone will wonder."

"I don't impose my family on you. I can't see why you don't do the same."

"You don't have a family. At least not like ours."

"Precisely because we don't bore ourselves stiff with unnecessary ritual."

"Mummy's Silver is hardly an unnecessary ritual. Sometimes, darling, you can be very crass."

"But I can't stand Mummy and Mummy can't stand me. What earthly good is it to both of us if I turn up?"

"That isn't true for a start. Mummy would quite like you if you gave her the chance."

"Mummy would feed me to the Doberman Pinscher if I gave her the chance."

"Hugo, you're impossible!"

"All I'm suggesting is that you and I are better off if we don't keep getting on top of each other."

Antonia sniffed loudly. "You were quite pleased to get on top of me half an hour ago." She tossed her heavy mane of hair and pulled the bedclothes to one side. Her nakedness was splendid in the undersea gloom of his bedroom with the blue curtains drawn. He watched as she pulled on her pants. She caught his eye with a malicious sidelong glance. "Just time to hurry down the road and catch Father O'Flaherty before he shuts up shop for the night. 'Father, forgive me, I've been up to no good again.'" Hugo always denied mentioning what they did in bed when he went to Confession but this was not quite true as Antonia may have suspected. She carried on in a cod Irish accent (mimickry was not one of her stronger points), "'Dat's all right, my son, you go away and say ten Hail Marys and be sure to tell me all about it again.'" Hugo yawned. She picked up a cushion and threw it at him. "Hugo, you are a *sod*. You never want to lift a finger for anyone!"

Lust was beginning to take the edge from his irritation and he reached across the rumpled bed to grab her. "There's something I'd quite like to lift for you now."

"Hugo! Don't be silly! I'm expected at the Frasers' ten minutes ago."

"It doesn't take me very long as you're never tired of reminding me."

"Hugo! Ouch! All right. Don't bite, I don't want marks all over my . . . Hugo . . ."

"Here's something for you to tell Mummy about next time you see her."

"Will you leave Mummy out of it! Oh Hugo, that's nice."

"It gets nicer," he whispered and for a little while there were no problems to worry about. She reminded him of one of them though afterwards, as she sprawled in his arms apparently trying to rip a mole from his arm with her fingernail. "I suddenly remembered," she said matter-of-factly, "I never asked how you got on with my little Jew and his miracle housekeeper."

"Ouch, Antonia, must you do that? It isn't painted on, you know. I didn't get on with him at all. He was away. I got on with his beautiful daughter instead. *Ouch!*"

"I had one on my shoulder and I got if off just like this. I'm sure I could get this off too. Mind, it left a bit of a mark. Keep *still*! Is his daughter beautiful? He isn't, you know."

"Yes, she is. She's about twelve. Well, sixteen anyway. Er — seventeen, I think, actually. Antonia, will you stop doing that, please?"

"I'm not really hurting, am I? You men are such cowards. But anyway you met the mad Italian housekeeper and heard all about the vision?"

"No, I didn't. She'd gone out for the afternoon. I don't think she liked the idea of talking to me."

"What? So you went all the way down there, and there was no one at home?"

"Except the daughter."

"Trust a Jew," said Antonia. "Trust a Jew to cock it up. But you enjoyed yourself instead talking to the beautiful daughter?"

"Antonia, I told you, she was fifteen."

"In that case she's definitely grown younger in the last few minutes. Seventeen is what you said then."

"Fifteen, sixteen, seventeen, what's the difference? At any rate she was a schoolgirl."

"Oh, a *schoolgirl*," said Antonia heavily. "Listen, darling, I must go. Could you chuck my bra? I'll ring tomorrow. And just think about Mummy's Silver Wedding will you, and try to bring yourself to say yes."

"Antonia, I've said . . ."

"I know what you've said. I'm sick of hearing what you've said. And could you just reach over for my sweater? No, all right, I'll get it. Oh, Hugo, I'm *sorry*. Did I squash them? I didn't mean to."

Carmen looked at the door, through which Mr Painscastle had just departed. Her first reaction had been to laugh, then to tell him to bugger off. But for some reason she had listened in silence, and now she was alone, images began to crowd upon her. She remembered the blue-sashed processions winding down to the Lourdes grotto, the baskets of strewn petals, the singing. *Thrown on life's surge, we claim thy care.* . . . They had prayed in their high young voices that they were sinners and needed saving. Sinners! They had hardly known what the word meant, supposing it to be something to do with coughing in Mass or eating sweets in Lent. How innocent she was then, thought Carmen, and began to cry into her whisky. Now she was innocent no more and God was punishing her for it all right. . . . '*To Thee do we cry, poor banished Children of Eve, to Thee do we cry, mourning and weeping in this vale of tears.* . . .' It all meant nothing then, but here she was in the vale of tears. Was there any comfort to be had? Were there no comforts but the old comforts?

Mr Painscastle wanted her to go down to the common with them. Well, perhaps she would.

That night was another sleepless one for Sister Scholastica. Her eyes seemed filled with fine sand, and her back ached whichever way she lay. She tried to offer up the ache to Jesus, but it was not painful enough to be got rid of in that way. It was a small ache. Sister Scholastica was being defeated by a small ache.

When she tried to pray, the words scattered and slithered away from her. When she closed her eyes huge faces materialised on her retina, mouthing and laughing at her. As she drifted off to sleep, thoughts came and wrenched her awake.

She thought of Anne Marie, prostrated before the vision, the vision denied to her. She thought of Saint Teresa and the Love which swept her away.

She thought of Rachel Gold.

She remembered Rachel the last time she had given her a lesson, how Rachel had sat looking at her with her chin cupped in her hand, and how suddenly she had turned to say something with a smile to Milly. Why, thought Sister, should Rachel's face be coming before her, when she was trying to think of God?

And then, in the small hours, things seemed suddenly to fit together. Perhaps all this was God's intention. Perhaps He too had designs on Rachel, and had chosen Sister to be His instrument. Radiant and innocent, only one Love could be good enough for Rachel, only one life would suit her. . . .

Gently, and tenderly now, sleep was beginning to enfold her in its blessed embrace. She felt strangely at peace now, the calm that follows the tempest. And just before she drifted off, something else fell into place. There was a role for Rachel to play which would take her even closer to God, and closer to . . .

Sister Scholastica slept.

Chapter 11

On the dark common a crowd had already gathered in spite of the drizzle. Some held candles, although there was no hope of lighting them, others had torches. There were perhaps three hundred people there, mostly women, in dark coats and headscarfs. Who were they all? How had the message spread? But it had spread, and they were there to see the miracle.

Somewhere in the crowd was Carmen Carmichael in her moth-eaten fur with a red headscarf. Hugo was there too, feeling rather foolish in his Burberry and good shoes. A man stood at the edge of the crowd with a large placard: THE POPE IS ANTICHRIST.

Carmen was ushered to the front. Someone had a chair for her but she would not sit down. Suddenly the crowd shivered with apprehension. Hugo strained to see. But all he could make out was a pale solid child in a school mack being led forward. He lost sight of her for a moment as she took up her position before the hawthorn bush, but then edged his way determinedly forward. Using his elbows, he managed to get close to the front of the crowd. When the little girl went rigid and fell to her knees an excited shiver rippled through the crowd and everyone fell into a tense silence. But Hugo could see nothing except the trees and the darkness, the little girl and the sea of faces, hushed and ecstatic. The little girl seemed to be saying something, although he could not hear what. Light fell on her face, an upturned moon. Flashlights popped around her and people were held back. Hugo shivered with something more than the cold and damp. He wished he had not come.

"We are baffled," said Doctor Ranesh. "Also, of course, we are delighted — as who would not be. But bafflement is also there."

"I'm not baffled," said Carmen. "I told you why, didn't I?"

"I must tell you, Miss Carmichael, that this is not an explanation for us doctors. Miracles are not our business. We do not think of things in such terms."

"Then in what terms do you think of something like this, may I ask?"

"Oh, Miss Carmichael, in very uncertain terms. But you see these things do happen and sometimes there seems to be no explanation. Remission is the word we would rather use. And I must tell you, such remissions may only be temporary, they may not last."

"Six weeks ago you say I'm not responding to treatment, and now you say I'm cured. And yet you're still standing there with a long face."

"Pardon, Miss Carmichael, I did not say cured. It would be too early to say cured. For the moment shall we say that the tumour appears to have retreated. Perhaps in six months, a year, we can begin to say cured."

"You doctors! Why must you be so cautious?"

"Caution is our job. We are not happy to raise someone up and then drop them down again bump. I should not like you to be disappointed later."

"Well, I'll tell you something," said Carmen. "Our Lady certainly isn't going to let me down bump. This is a *miracle*. She's cured me, and that's it."

But afterwards, as she walked down the street in her moth-eaten fur, she could not help smiling, so that people seeing her must have thought she was mad. In the butcher's shop a tiny plaster pig with a striped apron and a string of salmon pink sausages bowed cheerily beneath a boater. She felt like bowing back. The rich unbearable red of a pyramid of apples made her want to cry. Colours! Such colours there were in the world! A splash of emerald chiffon to make a sari, a strand of light bulbs winking and flashing, a tray of buns oozing cream and blood-red jam, bilberry-mauve mussels and sunset-colour haddock! What a rich, charged, gloriously overstocked place the world was! And it was all hers now to bite and chew and crunch, to her heart's content!

But there was Someone she must not forget to thank in her joy! Yes, there He was, after all. He had not forgotten her, though she had long forgotten Him. The sparrow had almost fallen, but He had reached out for it just in time.

The church was dark and gloomy. How cold it seemed, what a sad house! She emptied her purse into the collection box while the Virgin and Saint Antony stared down at her with their black beady eyes. Five pounds, ten, what did it matter? She would create such a blaze as had never before been seen. Feverishly she pressed candles into the dozen empty spikes before the Virgin but somehow that was not enough, so she squashed candles in between, balancing them precariously on the rack. One fell to the floor, but never mind, there were plenty more. She pushed them into the Virgin's coldly clasped hands, at her feet, in her arms. The light flickered and spurted and settled down to shine like a mass of diamonds. Candles everywhere, all lit up. More? Why, there must be more! Here were two on the altar, big, stiff and yellow. And more in the vestry, in a box marked, 'Lights: Extra Pure Produce of Spain'. Her hand was shaking so much that they kept falling over and splashing her hand with hot wax. It all looked so wonderful. If there had been a bell to ring, she would have rung that too. And if she had her paints, she would have left a mural charging over those bare walls, a huge mural bursting with life and celebration. How wonderful life was! And to think it had taken her all those years to appreciate it!

Father Joyce came into the empty church later to find his entire stock of candles blazing away. Some had fallen to the floor. Even the big altar ones now had stalactites of wax dripping from the side. Wax was everywhere. It took him a good fifteen minutes to put all of them out, and another hour on his hands and knees to scrape up all the molten wax.

★

"It doesn't look as though Mr Thomson is going to come," said Mr Blackaby.

"You know these Fatima people," said Mrs Evans-Blow. "They go on as though there's only ever been one apparition in the world. They're so jealous of *their* vision."

"If the London Friends refuse to co-operate," said Mr Painscastle, "then we'll just have to go ahead without them."

"A pity, but there you are," agreed Mrs Evans-Blow.

"I think it's such a shame," said Miss Finch. "And I think it's a shame about Mrs Kelly, too."

"Now we won't start all that again if you don't mind."

"Mrs Kelly isn't a bad soul," put in sister Mahony.

"No one's saying that, Sister," said Mr Painscastle sternly, "but we feel that this is too important for Mrs Kelly to monopolise."

"I know that, but . . ."

"But what, Miss Finch?"

"Nothing," said Miss Finch in a tiny voice. "Nothing."

"I think we'd better proceed with business. Everyone all right?"

"Yes."

"Mrs Evans-Blow?"

"Ready!" sang Mrs Evans-Blow, wielding her shorthand pencil.

"I shall start. The first meeting of the Society of Our Lady of the Common, November . . ."

"I really think we should find some other name," murmured Mr Blackaby. "It sounds like a football fan club."

"What do the rest of you feel about that?"

"I agree with Mr Blackaby."

"So do I."

"Then our first resolution will be to find another name. Shall we all think up some ideas and bring them to the meeting next week?"

"But how am I to write my minutes? I can't write minutes for a society that has no name."

"Let's call it a study group for the time being."

"Study Group for the Society of Our Lady of the Common? Study Group for the Apparitions of Our Lady on the Common?"

"Study Group provisionally called The Society for Our Lady of the Common," said Mr Blackaby firmly.

"Am I to write all that down?"

"Just put anything, my dear," said Miss Finch. "After all, we can sort everything out later."

"No," said Mr Blackaby. "We must do everything properly from the beginning. We don't want to be thought of as just a load of cranks."

"Which we will be."

"Which we will be," agreed Mr Blackaby. "So let's be as professional as possible."

"I think initials would be nice," put in Sister Mahony. "What about S.V.C.? Society for the Virgin of the Common?"

"Sounds like a venereal disease to me," said Mrs Evans-Blow. Sister Mahony looked shocked.

"But that is a very good idea," said Mr Painscastle. "An acronym that suggests simple dignity. Like M.A.R.Y."

"What about L.O.V.E.?" suggested Sister Mahony. "Light of the Blessed Virgin Enquiry Group."

"Properly speaking," said Mr Blackaby, "that would spell out LOTBVEG."

"I really think," said Mr Painscastle, "that we're wasting too much time on inessentials. Mrs Evans-Blow must just write down the provisional title and we'll think up a permanent name next week. Now we have far more important things to discuss. How we're going to arrange some sort of protection for the site, for example. Has anyone been there today?"

"I went this morning," said Sister Mahony. "I go every day now. I find it a very peaceful start to the day, but it was a disgrace. They've cleared everything away, flowers, candles, everything. And the hawthorn tree has been ripped almost to the ground."

"We should put something there that's too large to be taken away."

"But Our Lady herself has asked for a chapel on the site."

"A chapel, at the very least. A basilica, I would say."

"Now, now, Mrs Evans-Blow. We don't want to run before we can walk. A basilica is, as you say, what we should aim at in the future. But for the time being, the aim is just to protect the site and prevent further damage and desecration. Now, Miss Finch, I believe you were going to put the whole thing in motion?"

"Yes, I sent off a letter to the Planning Department yesterday, requesting permission for a permanent shrine."

"We can't expect a reply for some time, of course. The wheels of the Town Hall . . ."

"And it's no mystery what they will say. They'll turn down Miss Finch's request flat."

"Of course they will at this stage. We expect that. But we must go through the correct form. We will receive their refusal and then mount the next stage of our campaign."

"What about the legal problems of building on common land?"

"I have a cousin who's a lawyer," said Mr Blackaby. "I'll put it to him."

"But meanwhile the site is being vandalised."

"What about a permanent patrol? Half a dozen of us there all the time. It shouldn't be too hard to arrange. After all, we've generated a lot of sympathy."

"But *all* the time? Day and night?"

"*I'm* not spending the night on the common," shuddered Mrs Evans-Blow. "All sorts of things . . ."

The doorbell rang.

"Now, who . . ." said Miss Finch.

"Perhaps Mr Thomson's had a change of heart."

But it was Carmen.

"I'm sorry I'm late," she said. "I've been walking around in a . . . oh, such wonderful news!"

"Well?" said Sister Scholastica. She had caught Rachel on the stairs outside the chapel. Rachel looked up at the nun's pale rigid face. There was no expression in the blue eyes; it was like looking into a mask.

"Hallo, Sister." Rachel attempted a smile.

"You seem very pleased with yourself today," said Sister Scholastica curtly. Rachel thought, as she had been thinking for some days, of Hugo: thin and fair, and somehow *vulnerable*, sitting on her parents' big sofa, and asking, so nicely, all about her feelings, in a way that no one had ever done before. She was full of excitement she could not quite define. Now, seeing Sister Scholastica, it was like having cold water thrown over her.

". . . which surprises me," Sister Scholastica went on, "after the essay which you had the temerity to hand in the other day."

"The essay? On Herodotus?"

"I see you retain a vague memory of the subject."

"What about the essay?"

"What about it, Rachel? Only that it was just about the worst thing I've ever read on the subject. A spider given the run of a pot of ink might have produced something better."

Rachel flushed angrily. "Sister, that's not fair!"

"Isn't it?"

"I wrote it in a bit of a hurry, but it really wasn't that bad."

Sister Scholastica did not reply. The comforting image of Hugo was fast vanishing from Rachel's mind. A cold shiver ran through her, as though Sister Scholastica was trying to . . . what? As though she was trying to bond them together with something cold and dead, something that resonated of empty ruins and bleak deserted spaces. What did Sister want from her? Why did she keep a special set of rules just for Rachel? Why couldn't she let her be?

Chapter 12

From Mrs Kelly to Hugo

Dear Mr Swann,
 Thank you for your letter, saying you wish to interview my daughter Anne Marie, well you can come to the house at 3.30 pm next Saturday afternoon (The first). As you know we have Incurred a good deal of expence due to the Apparitions of Our Blessed Lady so I must ask you for a Fee, twenty-five pounds please *not* a cheque which you can bring with you when you come.

Yours faithfully,
K. Kelly (Mrs)

From Sister Scholastica of the Seven Sorrows Convent to Hugo

Dear Mr Swann,
 Reverend Mother Mary Dymphna asks me to thank you for your letter in which you express an interest in the story of Anne Marie Kelly. Unfortunately as this matter is at present under investigation by the diocesan Bishop we regret that we are unable at present to comply with your wishes for an interview.

Yours sincerely,
Sister Scholastica,
A.M.D.G.

Anonymous to Father Bob Joyce

 This is what I think of you Father, it is not right of you not to support Anne Marie Kelly who is a Saint and Our Lady will strike you down for your hard-heartedness. Call yourself a Christian you are not even good enough for a Jew. . . .

From the 'Sunday World', November 25

Pretty Anne Marie Kelly, 13, looks no different from any other ordinary teenager. The walls of the bedroom she shares with her sister, Lisa, 10, are covered with pictures of her favourite pop group, Duran Duran. Only a small statue of the Madonna of Lourdes over the mantelpiece tells you that this is a devout Roman Catholic household. Yet over the head of this soft-spoken, unassuming girl, an extraordinary storm has been raging which has shaken the Roman Catholic world to its foundations.

To the Editor of the 'South London Herald'

Sir,
Can nothing be done about the persistent and offensive invasion of our public spaces by so-called Roman Catholic 'visionaries'? Those of us who regularly use the facilities of the common for exercising our dogs and other leisure activities have of recent weeks found ourselves considerably restricted by these lunatics, some of whom even don official-looking badges and try to move us out of our way when we are going about our legitimate business. . . .

Sir,
I am appalled by the lack of coverage your paper has given to the marvellous events of recent weeks on the common. Surely, even you, as a non-Catholic, can see the importance of these events and the significance of the message which Our Lady wishes to tell the world. . . .

Sir,

So our local common is to become another Lourdes! Well, with youth unemployment running at sixteen per cent in the borough, surely we should all, Roman Catholics and others, look on this as a marvellous opportunity to bring a much needed breath of life into our decaying economic system. . . .

Memo to the Chief Planning Officer from the Town Clerk

Quite honestly, all I can say is try to hold them off as long as possible. After all, this is likely to be another nine-days wonder just like the skateboard park, and remember we didn't give way on that one either! Incidentally, the mother-in-law is an RC, so you can imagine some of the pressures I've been under at home these last weeks!

Might you be free for a round of golf next Saturday? It's been a long time since the last one.

From Dr Parker to Dr Ranesh

It is as you say, most bewildering. Might there have been any question of mistake over the X-rays? It could be worth a double-check. But the condition does appear to have retreated, and very suddenly. While it is, of course, too soon to talk of a cure, it is certainly extraordinary. Incidentally, I have just turned down a pressing request to appear on a TV chat show and I suggest you do the same if approached. Even with anonymity guaranteed, I feel it would be most unwise at this stage to comment one way or another in public.

From Rachel Gold to Hugo

I hope I'm not being a nuisance, but I found some of Anne Marie Kelly's old school books when I was helping to clear out a cupboard at school and I wondered if they might be of any use to you. You said any time I was near the King's Road to give you a call. Well, we have a school holiday on the 7th and I wondered if I might not drop the books in then. Do say if it's a nuisance. It was most interesting to meet you last week and I'm sorry Angelina wasn't there. She's still sulking actually!

With best wishes,
Rachel Gold

Chapter 13

"Aren't you leaving it all a little late?" asked Sister Imelda over lunch.

Sister Scholastica gave her an icy glare. "Everything is under control."

"I'm sure it is that," said Sister Mark. "I'm sure it's all under *control*."

"Sister Walpurgis has already started on the costumes and Miss Cooper has had the choir rehearsing for some weeks. I'm surprised you haven't been aware of it, Sister." Sister Scholastica sliced her bread into eight neat pieces, and began to eat them very slowly.

"You know me," said Sister Imelda, "I never notice anything until it's right under my nose. And under my nose there has been a distinct impression of not very much happening."

"Sister Oliver Plunkett used to make such a show," said Sister Aloysius wistfully.

"Sister Oliver Plunkett had her own ways of doing things. I have mine." Sister Scholastica laid a postage stamp of cheese on a square of bread and raised it to her lips.

"I used to love Sister Oliver's Tableaux!" sighed Sister Aloysius. Sister Oliver Plunkett had left the convent two years earlier to become a medical missionary. Behind her, she left memories of the Christmas *Tableaux Vivants*, one of the highlights of the year at the Seven Sorrows, and a fat file full of instructions for their production. Last year nothing had happened. This year, without anyone quite realising how, Sister Scholastica had taken charge. Everyone could remember ebullient Sister Oliver Plunkett bounding around the school in the days of the production radiating excitement. Sister Oliver Plunkett's Tableaux had been a triumph. How could Sister Scholastica compete?

"Have you decided on the cast yet?" asked Sister Mark.

"I hope to put the list on the board on Friday."

"But surely you can give us a tiny hint?"

Sister Scholastica began to perform a precision cutting job on a tomato, and considered. "Well," she said, "I thought Margaret Knox for Saint Joseph. Elinor will do for the Archangel Gabriel provided she does something about her hair. For the Three Wise Men, I thought Betsy Chin, Kate Taylor and Philomena Clarke."

"Oh dear Philomena!" enthused Sister Aloysius. "I can just imagine that jolly black face beneath a turban!"

"You'd better not let Philomena hear you say that," said Sister Mark. "You won't get her to play anything if you talk about her jolly black face."

"I know. They can be so touchy," said Sister Aloysius. "I can't think why. I keep telling them it doesn't matter; we're all God's children, black, white or green."

"Green?" said Sister Charles Borromeo. "Green? I had no idea that there were to be Martians too in the kingdom of Heaven."

"Are you sure Philomena will want to play Balthazar?" said Sister Imelda. "Won't she feel that you're making her a — what is it they call it now — a ticket?"

"I think you mean a token," said Sister Scholastica tartly. "Most likely she will, but token or not, she'll have to swallow her racial pride and do it. There's no one else. Linda Wilson is far too young, and that Nigerian girl too stupid." Sister Scholastica swallowed two pieces of cheese in quick succession as though they were Philomena's racial pride.

"What about Our Lady herself?" asked Sister Aloysius. "We haven't mentioned the most important person."

"Maybe young Anne Marie could be persuaded to arrange a personal appearance," said Sister Mark, but this was going too far. "*Really*, Sister!" said Sister Aloysius.

Sister Scholastica was seen to be looking casually out of the window. "I thought Rachel Gold for Our Lady," she said, taking advantage of the *frisson* caused by Sister Mark's bad taste.

"*Rachel?*"

"Why not Rachel?"

"But Sister," said Sister Imelda, "Rachel Gold is *Jewish*."

"Oh?" said Sister Scholastica coldly. "Wasn't Our Lady something of the sort too?"

"But under the circumstances . . ."

"I should have thought a nice Catholic girl could have been found to play Our Blessed Lady," said Sister Aloysius, nodding sagely.

"I really can see no reason . . ." said Sister Scholastica.

"Here we are, ladies," said Sister Benedict, coming in with a great steaming dish.

"Chocolate sponge! Yummy!" said Sister Mark.

"Now, who's serving? Don't forget a piece for Rev Muv. She's having hers on a tray in her room today. Poor dear, she's overwhelmed. She's struggling with a letter to the Bishop over you-know-who."

"If that girl had any idea of the trouble she's caused. . . ."

"Oh, I think she has *every* idea."

"Don't we get any *custard*?" said Sister Mark.

"And what about Anne Marie Kelly?" said Sister Aloysius. "Do we have a tiny wee part for Anne Marie in our festivities?"

"No."

"Not even a shepherd boy? Or a fat little angel?"

Sister Scholastica permitted herself an icy smile. "No Sister," she said "we do not."

Father Mack stood in the doorway, a huge lurching mass in the solemn black of his robes, a dark unstable mountain, breathing, too, some fairly sulphurous fumes over Hugo.

Hugo, who had not seen nor heard from him since that terrible dinner party, stared in surprise.

"Dear boy," the priest said thickly, "dear, dear boy." He swayed a little and might have fallen but Hugo put out a hand to steady him.

"You'd better come in."

"I can see what you're thinking, and you are right," said Father Mack, taking two steps forward with a belch which rendered him briefly pop-eyed. "I am — drunk — and that most appallingly, most dreadfully."

"Come and sit in the living room, Father."

A little Georgian table (bought with his first royalties) juddered nervously in the priest's wake and a Staffordshire milkmaid followed. Hugo tried to steer him safely past precious obstacles but the huge bulk was resistant. Eventually though, Father Mack found the mantelpiece and leaned heavily against it with no more damage than to send a shower of invitation cards fluttering to the floor.

"'Oh the mind . . .'" intoned Father Mack heavily, "'the mind' — excuse me — 'has mountains. Hold them cheap. . . .' Do you remember how we used to read Hopkins together? 'Hold them cheap may who ne'er hung there.' Old Hopkins knew all right, James, Simon, sorry, I mean Hugo. Do you have a drop of whisky for an old man?"

"I think under the circumstances, a little black coffee . . ."

"You think I've had too much already. A drunk priest, a whisky priest — excuse me — and of course you are right. I have had too much, oh dear boy, how I have had too much. These last strands of man in me, Hugo, they have been pulled beyond endurance!"

"I'll put the kettle on," said Hugo.

"No, no coffee. I don't want coffee; shan't drink it. That whisky — I'm sure you have a drop somewhere."

"I do," said Hugo, "only it's Glenmorangie, so mind you appreciate it on me, Father."

"Ah, yes, you always had a sense of the best, Hugo, that was why I came to you in the dark night of my soul. Give me your Glenmorangie, my son, and you shall be paid back a thousand-fold."

"Well, all right," said Hugo reluctantly. He fetched the bottle and two glasses. The drink he poured for Father Mack was very small.

"Bless you for your kindness. It shall be repaid." The priest cradled the glass in his big hands. "The finest on earth. Let's make it even finer, shall we?"

"Father?"

"Silver and gold have I none, but what I have I give you. Let us remember the words of Our Blessed Lord, who the day before He suffered took whisky — no sorry, took wine, and with his eyes lifted up to heaven, to God His almighty Father, giving thanks, did bless and give to His disciples, saying . . ."

"Father, I think . . ."

"Did bless and give to His disciples, saying . . ."

"*Father!*"

But the priest now had turned to face him and steadying his back against the marble mantelpiece held up the glass in his two hands so that it caught the light. "*Hic est enim calix sanguinis mei novi et aeterni testamenti, mysterium fidei, qui pro vobis et pro multis effundetur in remissionem peccatorum.* As often as you shall do these things you shall do them in remembrance of Me."

There was a long silence. Father Mack lowered the glass and stared at it. A piece of coal fell down in the fire with a crash.

"I think you went a bit far there, Father."

"But it can't be undone, Hugo. What's done is done. The miracle can never be unperformed. Take ye and drink, Hugo, the best whisky you'll ever know."

He tried to thrust the glass at Hugo, lurching so that whisky trickled down Hugo's shirt, but Hugo sidestepped quickly and the priest drank it down himself. When he had finished he threw the empty glass to the ground where it rolled away on the carpet and said, "I am leaving the Church, Hugo. I have had enough."

"Leaving?"

"I am leaving."

"You can't mean that."

"It's true. I mean it most certainly. In vino veritas or in my case in malto, and the truth is I've had enough of the old bitch. I've watched her change her coat from virgin to harlot these last few years and I have watched dumbly until at last I can take no more."

"But Father, you love the Church. It's your life."

"Loved, Hugo, loved. The Church I loved no longer exists. Instead of a rock, I see only a quicksand. Instead of marble, only plastic. No more, Hugo, no more. I shall find a flat and get a job and I shall let the flesh have its way. I shall drink and gluttonise and lust . . ." He veered very close to Hugo who pulled himself away in alarm. "I shall go to the devil, and damn me, as indeed it will, I shall enjoy it. And now, having leaned on your lovely mantelpiece, I shall stagger out into the night and find a taxicab and return to scandalise everybody. . . . How I've longed all these years for that sweet young flesh, those moist lips, those plump bottoms. But no more longing, Hugo, no more longing. . . ."

As he staggered through the front doorway and out into the night, Hugo could still hear him intoning loudly down the street, "*Introibo ad altare Dei. Ad Deum qui laetificat juventutem meam* . . ."

"Nonsense, my girl," said Sister Scholastica. "You'll do it perfectly."

"But I can't," wailed Rachel. "Sister, I can't." Lights, the stage, all eyes upon her! Oh God!

"You *can't*?" said Sister. "Can't? Elinor's only too pleased to be asked. Margaret's delighted. Kate Taylor is perfectly happy to oblige. What's so special about Miss Rachel Gold that what's good enough for everyone else isn't good enough for her?"

"Sister you don't understand! It's not like that."

"Then what is it like?"

"I'd be . . . embarrassed. I'd spoil it for everybody else."

They were alone in the blue and white needlework room with long formica tables and presiding statue of Saint Anne, where Rachel, the only girl in the sixth to study Greek, had her lesson. Rachel's eyes were bright and intense, as though conflicting feelings swam about inside her head like tiny vivid tropical fish. On the formica table somebody had written in felt-tip pen, 'Sex rules OK signed B.W.'

Sister ran a finger over it distractedly before returning to Rachel with a sudden unexpected smile. "My dear, I don't want to make you do something that you find offensive. But I would like it — truly — if you would take this part. After all, no speaking is involved and I will tell you exactly what to do. Please try and tell me what your objections are. Is it the religion?"

"Religion?"

"Is it difficult for a Jewish girl to play Our Lady?"

This had scarcely occurred to Rachel in the variety of horrors that the nun's words had evoked in her. "Oh no, Sister."

"Would your parents object?"

"I don't think so."

"Then what?" The nun leaned forward, her eyes behind her thick glasses suddenly as piercing as laser beams. "Rachel, you're not trying to tell me that there's . . . some other reason why you should find it inappropriate to play the Blessed Virgin?"

Rachel suddenly caught her meaning and blushed in horror. "*No*, Sister!"

The nun let a small smile cross her face. Her voice was all gentleness now, all soft persuasion. "Then *what* is it, my dear?"

But how could you explain it, that awful clutching in the stomach when you thought of yourself so publicly exposed on a stage, everybody looking at you. No. Oh no.

"Rachel?"

Last night Rachel had had a row with her mother — they happened quite often these days — and her mother had called her silly, vain and unhelpful. She tried hard not to be any of these things; all she wanted was for people to like her. But it was all . . . impossible. Such a muddle.

"Nothing. It's just . . ."

"Just . . . ?"

"Just . . . You know, life."

Life? From somewhere in the back of Sister Scholastica's memory that word set up a small anxious echo. Life! The little echo quavered, struggled for existence and then died away. "*Life*, Rachel?"

But Rachel had run out of excuses. "All right," she said dully. "I'll do it. I'll play the part."

"Is there a drop more vino, darling, for a thirsty girl?" asked Antonia, holding out her glass.

He had cooked a most delicate salmon trout with fennel and a salad of chicory and radicchio in walnut oil vinaigrette, followed by an apricot mousse, and Antonia had devoured it all very fast, talking the while of the adventures of some friend and his Aston Martin in Norfolk. "Apparently it was the big end. Have you any idea what a big end is, darling, it always sounds obscene to me, but anyway there he was in the middle of nowhere at half past two in the morning with his big end gone and what on earth was he to *do*?"

"Go by train next time," said Hugo shortly. Really he could have made baked beans on toast and she would have devoured it just as happily.

"Actually, you'd like Ben," she said happily, swigging down another glass of Berry Brothers' best *Muscadet*. "He used to be a Cistortionate monk for five years."

"I think you mean Cistercian."

"Well, whatever. He was one, anyway. I don't know what good it did him, he's apparently *the* most amazingly randy beast now. Don't worry darling, I haven't had personal experience, but my friend Camilla says he just has this permanent *hard-on*."

"So you think I'd like him, do you?"

"Not like that, silly. I mean to talk to. Yes, I really think I'll have to have you two to dinner together some time. He's very funny about all the things he had to do as a monk. You could swap notes about your Catholic upbringings."

"Catholics hate swapping notes with other Catholics. They like to feel they're quite alone in the world with their dreadful experiences. Besides, I *like* being a Catholic, thank you."

"You're being awfully prickly today, darling, have you had a bad time? You can't have had such a bad day as I did; the catalogue was fucked up by the printers so *moi* had to spend the entire day trailing round London trying to find someone else to do it in the time. I'm knackered, I can tell you."

"You *poor* thing."

"Don't sound so superior. I *do* work hard, you know."

"I never said you didn't."

"Just because I don't sit on my arse all day thinking about Literature, you think I'm some sort of inferior species."

"Antonia, you're being very silly now."

"Silly?" she cried. "Silly? How can *you* say *I'm* silly?"

"Very easily. You're silly. You're being silly now."

"And you of course are so amazing. Such a perfect example of manhood."

"And what's that supposed to mean?"

"Come on, darling, you know perfectly well. I mean if you *like* being fucked by an express train, then yes, I suppose you're wonderful."

"Oh? And has it never occurred to you that perhaps you're not the great *femme fatale* you imagine?"

"No one else has complained."

"And there've been plenty of takers, I know."

"Oh I *see!*" she cried. "I might have known you'd come out with that sooner or later! We're back on the old double standard, aren't we? Poor old Antonia, no better than she should be."

"Please don't twist everything I say."

"I don't need to. *You* twist perfectly well for both of us! You're the most twisted person I've met."

"Oh really, Antonia."

"You're so obsessed with your bloody *soul* and your bloody *self*."

"And you of course aren't obsessed with yourself?"

"See! You're doing it again. At least *I* don't spend all my time boring everybody rigid with my spiritual crises."

"Do you find me so boring? Oh dear. I assumed I could confide in you."

"Confide! You just want some idiot to listen while you babble on! I'm sick of it!"

"I'm sorry to hear it, Antonia."

"Do you know, when I first met you, I was really keen on you; I even thought, for Christ's sake, I might want to *marry* you. And because you were always going on about Catholics, well, I thought I'd better go along and find out something about them. It was the least I could do, I thought, for the man I loved. Huh! That was a laugh. So I went along to the bloody church, the Holy Knickers or whatever it calls itself, and I sat there, listening."

"Oh really? And were you edified by this experience?"

"Was I hell? Do you know, I have never seen so many bored, half-asleep people in my life, and that included the priest. I thought, damn it, these people are supposed to be talking about the most sacred bloody mysteries of life and death, they're going on about eternity and things like that, and it was just like he was handing out dollops of cold mashed potato! Honestly, darling, I'm not religious, but it made my blood freeze. And I thought afterwards, God, that's what Hugo finds so bloody marvellous, that's what he does every week. And I thought, if that's all there is to it, then what about all the other stuff he goes on about? How do I know that isn't all a load of bullshit too?"

Chapter 14

The following day, he was sure Antonia would phone and make it up with him. They had argued before but in the past she had always been the one to say, "Well, Hugo, you idiot, can we be friends again, please?" But the morning passed and nothing happened. The quarrel — had it been a quarrel? — was having a bad effect on his work. No one understood how delicate was the equilibrium of a writer, how easily disturbed. It was really most unfair of her to upset him like this.

Father Mack had let him down too. Now one of his purest memories had been polluted. He could never again think of that wonderful year of faith without remembering the drunken priest's blasphemous mutterings over the whisky glass. The empty glass posed another problem for him the following morning. After all, Father Mack was still a priest, and as a priest he had spoken the sacred words over the Glenmorangie. Now the glass was empty, but you could hardly fling a vessel that had held Christ's blood, however briefly and blasphemously, into a bowlful of Fairy Liquid with the breakfast plates. Ideally it should have been destroyed, but the dustbin was not a suitable place either, and anyway it was a good piece of crystal which he did not want to lose. In the end he put it back on the shelf with the other glasses, moving them around so that he might forget which one it was. A letter arrived in the post from Father Mack the next day, sober but not entirely repentant, saying that he would probably try to join some High Anglican community. Fortunately no mention was made of the pleasures of plump buttocks.

Later that morning, though, something more encouraging happened. His agent telephoned in great excitement: a lunchtime television programme wanted to run a story on Anne Marie's visions and they needed what he called a 'tame Catholic' to give his views. Hugo began to argue all the reasons why someone like himself could really not be expected to give instant opinions on so sensitive a subject, but in the end, though sounding reluctant, he agreed. There was a nasty electricity bill to be paid.

But still Antonia did not phone.

The following day, he set off for his interview with Mrs Kelly. However, this proved to be a disappointment: Mrs Kelly had become an accomplished manipulator, and his own skills were not enough to get more information from her than she was prepared to give. Anne Marie, whom he was allowed to see only briefly, was silent and inarticulate. He came away from the interview depressed and uneasy, with a sense only of the bleakness of the Kellys' lives.

But this failure determined him to follow up the one glimpse of an interesting story that had emerged. Mrs Kelly had spoken of the hostility of the local priest, and Hugo decided to pay Father Joyce a visit.

He saw the squat ugly church of purple brick with a shudder, reminding him again, if he needed reminding, of the horrors that lay beyond the Oratory. The church was empty except for a little nun who was cleaning out a hymn book cupboard. Yes, she said, Father Joyce was in, and she directed him to the flat.

Father Joyce opened the door and looked at Hugo in surprise. Hugo could not know how rare it was for him to get a visitor. But the surprise was soon replaced by an expression of friendly receptiveness. "And what can I do for you?" he asked. Hugo noted a boyish face that nevertheless was considerably older than it first appeared. Father Joyce saw Hugo's incongruous Chelsea smartness, the Burberry raincoat and polished shoes. Hugo wondered briefly whether the priest might be homosexual; Father Joyce wondered the same thing about Hugo, which may have accounted for a slight awkwardness that was in the air as the priest invited Hugo into his living room.

Nevertheless, he beamed encouragingly at Hugo. "What about a spot of coffee?" "Most kind," murmured Hugo. Soon the priest returned with a tray. "Sugar?" he asked. "Biccy?" The coffee was terrible — milk and Nescafé all boiled up together. "It's most kind of you to let me disturb you like this," said Hugo, swallowing it down.

"No trouble," said the priest. "We like to be of help where we can. Though I warn you, there isn't too much I can say. Everything's under wraps while the Bishop investigates. I had to turn away a fellow working for the *Universe* the other day."

"I'm not a journalist," said Hugo. "I'm a writer actually. This is a new departure for me."

"Oh, a writer," said Father Joyce, sounding impressed. "I'm very fond of a good book myself. Not that I get much time for reading." The words fell hollowly into what became a stiff silence. Hugo heard himself repeating, "It's awfully good of you . . ."

"So you're writing about . . ." said the priest at the same time, and they both laughed in embarrassment.

"I really came," said Hugo, trying to gather himself together, "to get your version of what you said to Mrs Kelly. She presents you as someone who is totally hostile to the idea of these visions, someone who doesn't believe Anne Marie at all. Can I ask you what your side of the story is?"

"Well," said the priest musingly, "Anne Marie's a nice enough girl and goodness knows the Kellys haven't had an easy time of it. But . . . Look, are you sure you won't have one of these biscuits? The nuns bake them for me every week, you know, and I haven't the heart to tell them that most of them don't get eaten. Hostile — what does Mrs Kelly mean by that? Did she say?"

"She suggested you wouldn't let them in your church."

"Correction. I won't preach the message of Our Lady as revealed to young Anne Marie in my church. The Kellys are as welcome to come as any. But Mrs K. chooses to interpret that as a ban. I think she rather wants it to be, if you ask me. A sense of martyrdom and all that. Only trouble is, she's taken quite a few of my parishioners along with her, and that's something I can't afford."

"Are your congregations small?"

"Small, and getting smaller. All your middle classes are off up at the convent where the singing's better and the incense gets flung about a bit more. The poor Irish that the church was built for have mostly moved on. So we're left with an odd sort of mixture, neither one thing nor the other. By the way, do feel free to smoke if you like."

"Thank you, I don't."

"Neither do I. Though sometimes when I look at that lot sitting in the pews on Sunday I wonder what I'm preserving my life for."

"You sound as though you'd be happier in another parish."

"There was a parish came up the other day I would have given my back teeth for. Brixton. The sort of place you can really get stuck into, you know. But they gave it to this bloke from Liverpool." His face sagged and suddenly he did not look boyish any more. But he soon cheered up. "Well, never mind. You didn't come here to hear me gassing on about my problems, did you? You want to hear about young Anne Marie. What else can I tell you? As I say, the integrity or otherwise of the young lady's really outside my range at the moment. The Bishop's got all that in tow. But anything else. . . ."

"What do you personally believe? Can I ask you that?"

"Aha. That's your six thousand dollar question, isn't it? Because you see, I don't really believe in any of them. Lourdes, Fatima, none of them. I think the kiddies believed they happened, but that's a different story. What, sending his mum down from heaven every so often to keep people in line? That isn't God's way."

"You think so?"

"If there's one thing the Almighty's keen on, it's the old free will. He didn't put us here to be ordered about by Him, even if we make a mess of things in the process. No, this is our life and we have to get on with it. No free gifts, no hand-outs. That's what I believe."

"No wonder your congregations are getting smaller."

"Come now, I don't actually stand up there in the pulpit on Sundays and say, look here, Bernadette was a nice girl, but she was off her rocker. I don't mess about with what people like to believe. You asked me what I believe and I've told you. You can put it in your article if you like, long as you tone it down a bit, so my last few parishioners don't go off me altogether."

"Book," said Hugo.

The priest looked dumbfounded.

"I'm writing a book," said Hugo, "not an article."

"Ah," said the priest. He did not seem very interested. They chattered politely for a few more minutes, covering the Tridentine Mass and the ecumenical movement in rather perfunctory fashion. The truth was, neither liked the other very much. Hugo suspected — rightly — that Father Joyce was the sort of priest who would not be averse to introducing guitar-playing nuns if it would whip the attendance figures up at Sunday Mass; Father Joyce suspected, also correctly, that Hugo was one of your incense-flinging Oratory types. Nevertheless, they parted with an appearance of amiability and cheery handshakes. Though when Hugo's footsteps had died away, Father Joyce went sadly into the living room, where the empty coffee cups and the untouched biscuits were still on their tray. This week the biscuits were pink and coconut. No wonder the Oratory type wouldn't touch them. He tried to eat one for the sake of nice Sister Mahony. Even she, though she was too polite to say anything, did not agree with the stand he had taken on Anne Marie. But what could you do? In the end, you could only follow your conscience, couldn't you? And his spoke out clearly enough. He sighed, and remembered the conversation he had just had with Hugo. "No free gifts," he repeated. "No visions. No easy way."

Hugo's appearance on the television show was a great success and to his surprise he enjoyed it. Beneath the lights and cameras something inside him glowed and expanded; he relaxed, smiled, answered questions, explained about visions and made a few gentle jokes as though he had been doing it for years. His agent was very excited too. Apparently the channel was looking for a new host for a book programme starting the following year, and since Hugo had shown himself to be a 'television natural' he was suddenly very much among the front runners. Hugo was not sure that he liked to be a television natural, but it gave a boost to his pride, which he was still much in need of after the row with Antonia. Meanwhile, he had arranged to met Rachel Gold for tea. Now he was beginning to feel like a real writer again, he told himself how she must be looking forward to it. He resolved to be especially nice to her.

Chapter 15

By the time she reached Sloane Square, Rachel was feeling quite nervous at her temerity. As if Hugo would really be interested in Anne Marie's old exercise books, which she had stolen from the child's desk one evening as the only pretext she could think of for seeing Hugo again. God, he must be *really bored* at the thought of being stuck with her for tea. There was nothing in the silly books anyway, except some grammar exercises over which the teacher had written 'This work must improve', and pages of dictated notes on Religious Knowledge.

The King's Road was full of people. They all seemed so self-possessed. Would she be like them one day? What were they thinking of her as she walked among them? Did they notice how unlike them all she was?

Peter Jones' restaurant was an odd place to be meeting someone and she found herself elbowed in the lift by some greedily determined old ladies. She scanned the sea of pastel hats and silvery hair and after a few brief panics (Suppose Hugo had forgotten? Suppose she had got the time wrong?) she was pleased to glimpse that slight, fair figure sitting at a table by the window, engrossed in a new paperback book, with a W. H. Smith bag beside him. When he saw her he waved and smiled and then stood up for her. None of the boys she knew would ever think of standing up. "Nice to see you again," he said with easy charm, as though they had been old friends. "Have you had a successful shop?" He smiled at the middle-aged waitress too, and she seemed to have fallen quite in love with him. "Shall I take your order now, Sir?" she asked politely.

"*Rather!*" he said with old-fashioned boyish enthusiasm.

"China or Indian, do you think, Rachel?"

"I don't mind." Oh God, how feeble!

"Then — China. All right?"

"Anything to eat, Sir? There's a lovely gâteau today."

"Gâteau, Rachel?"

A year ago she would have jumped at gâteau. But now — now, it would have choked her. "No, thank you."

"Then — I say," he said to the waitress with an air of conspiracy, "you wouldn't run to some cucumber sandwiches?"

"Cucumber sandwiches? I think we can rustle up some cucumber sandwiches for you, Sir."

"That would be lovely." And then he turned the beam of his attention on Rachel. "Now tell me about you. What sort of a week have you had?"

Father Bob Joyce was preparing his sermon for the following day when he heard the package falling through the letter box. It was the sound of running footsteps on the outside stairs that made his heart sink, but whoever it was was already out of sight when he looked out of the window. The parcel was crudely wrapped and had broken apart even before it hit the carpet. Was it from a Catholic, or from a Methodist or a Jehovah's Witness? He had received hate mail from just about every creed these last weeks. What more did God want of him?

Slowly, he went towards the kitchen to fetch floorcloths, newspaper and disinfectant.

Sister Scholastica had left the common room to escape the blare of football. The nuns had recently developed a passion for Brian Kennedy, East Ham's new striker, on the flimsy grounds that he was a Catholic and came from Tooting. Pictures of his big, hunky, brainless smile hung everywhere. Just now, Sister Mark was excited almost to ecstasy because he had scored his second goal. Sister Scholastica considered all this highly improper and had said so, but to little effect, so she took her pile of homework to be corrected to the library, the only place, apart from the chapel, where you could be sure of quietness these days. The convent had become so noisy since the relaxation of the rule; nuns who had once glided and whispered, now ran and shouted. Radios were played, telephones shrilled, ping-pong balls clattered, the television gabbled, and there was even talk, since they had become obsessed with it on late night programmes, of getting a half-size pool table.

On top of the pile of books was Rachel Gold's Greek translation. Sister looked for mistakes but the work was flawless.

A great shout broke out, travelling down the corridor, penetrating even the firmly shut library door. Sister Scholastica turned down her lips in distaste. Brian Kennedy had scored another goal.

"Really!" said Hugo, leaning across the table in interest. "Do you mean to tell me you've never read Herbert?"

"They prefer it when we read Catholic poets. They love Belloc and Chesterton and Hopkins." She felt a little out of her depth. Of course discussing poetry was what people did, intellectual artistic people like Hugo, but didn't it all feel a bit cold-blooded when you were actually doing it? She had imagined a scene exactly like this many times — talking about literature with some lovely man — but there was another conversation she craved to be having; though it was only because she was so stupid that the abstractions of poetry seemed unsatisfactory. She wanted — oh, she wanted to talk about *life*, she wanted to bare her soul, she wanted to probe Hugo's depths in return. If only he would ask her how she felt about something other than poetry, if only she didn't have to keep racking her brains to keep up with him!

"Will you have the last sandwich?" he asked. "No? Well. If you're sure. . . . It was most kind of you to get hold of these books for me. Are you sure they were only going to be thrown away? I tell you what, why don't you come to tea at the flat next Saturday and I'll lend you some books? I have a nice little edition of Crashaw too."

If only she could have said yes! "I'm afraid . . . I'm afraid I can't." For next Saturday was the last of the three evenings on which the *Tableaux Vivants* were to be shown, and she could not get out of that. "I can't . . ." Whatever happened, he must never know about those silly Tableaux, and her being the Virgin Mary! It was too embarrassing. Whatever happened . . . "I can't, I . . ."

But to her horror, she found herself telling him all about them. Oh God, why hadn't she kept her mouth shut?

"I think someone should do something."

"What do you suggest?"

Sister Mark shook her head. "Doesn't anyone else *see*? Isn't anyone else worried?"

"I really do think you're exaggerating, Markie."

"Exaggerating!"

"Sister Scholastica is a devout woman. We may not like it but you can't get away from it."

"Excuse me, but I don't think it's devout the way she behaves. I think she's going crazy."

"That's rather a strong word, isn't it?"

"Listen dears, I don't stay stuck in this convent all day. I go out in the world and I see what things are like. And believe me, Sister Scholastica's behaviour isn't *normal*."

"How isn't it normal?"

"She hardly eats a thing these days. Haven't you noticed? And she doesn't eat meat at all any more."

"But my dear Sister, this is *Advent*. Surely poor Sister Scholastica is allowed to fast during Advent."

"This has nothing to do with abstinence. I'm talking about an *illness*."

"Now there's a name for that, isn't there? mused Sister Aloysius. "I read about it in a magazine I confiscated from one of the girls."

"You're not trying to say that Sister Scholastica is anorexic?" said Sister Monica.

"Hooray. Ten out of ten, Sister."

"But that only happens to teenagers. Sister Scholastica is hardly that."

"There are so many things they talk about today," said Sister Aloysius. "Why when I was a girl, we just got on with it. No one worried about the state of our minds, and a good thing too, I think."

"Do you have anything else to prove your theory?"

"She washes her hands all the time. Haven't you noticed? It's just like Lady Macbeth."

"Lady *who*?" said Sister Aloysius looking up. "Oh, *Macbeth*."

"And if you move her work or her pen or her ruler a fraction of an inch out of line, she's like a cat on hot bricks till she's got everything back in place."

"She has a tidy mind. What's wrong with that?"

"Oh, this is hopeless," said Sister Mark.

"Then you must go and tell Reverend Mother if you're really worried. Gossiping to us won't do any good, you know."

"What use would that be? As far as Rev Muv's concerned, Sister Schol can do no wrong. I'd be wasting my time."

"Then you must bow to Reverend Mother's decision," said Sister Monica, gently reproving. "This may be the 1980s, as you're so fond of reminding us, but we have taken our vows of obedience, and they still count for something."

"Don't remind me," said Sister Mark. "I'm obedient till it comes out of my ears. But when I see something like this. . . . Oh well, what does it matter? I'm going to be fearfully late if I don't get a move on."

Rachel was in love! She had never known anything like it. All the clichés were true; she couldn't eat or sleep or work. Her head was hammering just as though it would burst. It was . . . it was dreadful, just thinking and thinking of somebody every minute of the day like this. Whoever said falling in love was wonderful?

And yet sometimes it was wonderful, when she just thought about him sitting there, across the flowery tablecloth, that fair intense *beautiful* face looking at her and smiling so kindly and asking such nice questions.

It had happened so suddenly. . . . One minute she was looking at him and then something went twang! like a racquet string snapping. All that earlier vague excitement had broken over her in a flood and washed her away. Had he noticed? Surely he must have done. Surely that great flood couldn't have passed him over unscathed. . . .

If only . . . what? What did she want from it all? She couldn't begin to ask herself.

The Bishop's room had never seen so many crimson robes. His housekeeper, Mrs Mottram, was quite flustered. "Dear!" she said. "It's just like when His Holiness came."

"We'll have a large pot of tea," said the Bishop, "and a plate of your nice shortbread biscuits if you can manage that, and then shut the door and leave us alone. And could you make sure there are some clean glasses on the tray, just in case. And tell Father Price that there are to be no — positively no — phone calls or interruptions until we've finished."

"She seems such a dear little girl," said Mrs Mottram. "Did you see her on the *News at Ten* last night? I thought she was ever so sincere."

"*Thank* you, Mrs Mottram, that'll be all," said the Bishop. The door closed behind her, and for a long time there was no voice to be heard but the Bishop's as he presented a summary of the latest events. At the end there was a long silence.

"It seems there's very little conclusive evidence either way," said a bishop who had come from the Midlands.

"Except the possible cancer cure," said another.

"Except the possible cancer cure. This, of course, is the believers' strongest card, and without it, I think this business would have made a considerably smaller impact."

"Has Monsignor spoken to Miss Carmichael and her doctors?"

"Indeed. And there seems to be no ambiguity there; the

woman was ill and now she's cured."

"An unexplained spontaneous cure. So we're talking about a miracle."

The Bishop nodded. "It's a matter of semantics of course, but you could say so. Shall we say, a strong case could be made for the miraculous nature of the cure by those in whose interests it is to make it."

"The local priest — is he still sceptical?"

"Very much so. In spite of being the victim of a peculiarly nasty campaign of harassment."

"He's a good priest, Father Joyce," said someone who knew him. "A very hard worker."

"It is, of course," said the bishop from the Midlands, "his privilege not to believe in miracles."

"Undoubtedly. But sometimes, you know, a little flexibility . . ."

"We have to concede that the increase in church attendance during this period has been remarkable. Father Ord, do you have the figures?"

Father Ord, a fresh-faced young man, looked at his notes. "In the Greater London area there has been an average increase of thirty per cent. This includes many churches in which attendance has doubled or more."

"And is that trend echoed in the whole country?"

"Certainly."

"Do you realise what this means? How many more practising Catholics there are in the country now than there were six months ago?"

"If it can only be maintained."

"I see no reason why not. There's bound to be some falling off, of course, but why should there not be lasting results from this wonderful surge?"

"I've been saying for many years," said the oldest bishop present, "That if everyone who was born a Catholic returns to the flock, that, combined with the natural trend of Catholics to have large families, would mean that by the end of the century we would be the majority Christian faith in this country. We don't even need to make converts."

"Nevertheless converts are being made. The Catholic Information Bureau reports a huge increase in those asking to be referred for instruction."

"God works in mysterious ways," said the bishop from the Midlands, raising an ironic eyebrow.

"Mysterious indeed. Anne Marie Kelly seems to be an odd person to single out for such an honour."

"Tell us," said the bishop from the Midlands, "you've had a greater chance than the rest of us to examine the evidence. May we ask what your own personal feelings on the matter are?"

The Bishop picked a bit of fluff from his sleeve before replying. "This is how I see it. Whether or not Our Lady actually *has* appeared on the common, there seems to be no doubt from the powerful excitement that this story has generated, that many people *believe* she has, and therefore the story might be said to have a symbolic truth. The same can be said for many episodes from the Bible, after all. We can accept Adam and Eve as a symbolic story, so why not this one too? After all, God who allows everything has allowed this story to take shape and to have an effect on His people, an effect which seems to us to be a most desirable one. So it seems to me that we may be just a little misguided to worry too much about its *literal* truth. A huge shoal of fish has come into our net at a time of despair and impiety. Are we going to let that shoal escape?"

There was a general murmur.

"And what about the girl's school?" said someone. "Are the nuns still unsympathetic?"

The Bishop shook his head sadly. "Between you and me, I've had about as much as I can take from those good ladies recently. I've had a plan for Seven Sorrows brewing for some time and I feel that now might be a good time to implement it. Ah well. Do you know, I think we have all earned ourselves a drop of whisky after that. What do you say?"

Chapter 16

What was Hugo doing here anyway? He wasn't sure himself, but here he was outside the gaunt Seven Sorrows on Thursday night just in time for the first showing of the Tableaux. So many schoolgirls acting angels and saints, was that it? Or just a chance to see inside the convent at last? Or Rachel playing the Virgin Mary; such beauty representing such holiness! At any rate, the idea had fixed itself so firmly in his mind after Rachel had first mentioned it that nothing would shake it, and so somehow here he was, among the Volvos and BMWs.

Antonia had still not made contact. Someone had told him that she had started going out again with Charles from Sotheby's or was it James the wine merchant? He told himself he did not care but the fact was that were he to meet James or Charles in the street he might well have punched James or Charles in the mouth. He could not be jealous — it was inconceivable. To be jealous of Antonia! It was his pride that was hurt, that was all.

Not far away, on the common, the rival attraction of another Virgin was pulling a large crowd too, but none of the Seven Sorrows parents would have gone in for such superstitious stuff. Catholics they might be, but they ruled the world and they knew it.

The night was dark and splendid; a big confident moon outlined the Gothic angularity of walls and roof. Hugo was caught in a press of conversations: "First gear went, then second, so there was nothing for it, she had to go." "When *do* Downside break up, do you know, Heather?" "No such luck, darling, she's only doing four CSEs, I'm afraid."

At the door a plump, smiling nun sold tickets ("Is your

daughter here tonight?" she said to a horrified Hugo) and two ungainly girls trying to flirt pressed a programme upon him ("Oh go on, Sir!"). In the corridor, familiar icons stared down at him, the Sacred Heart, Saint Joseph, Saint Dominic. The smell of school was almost lost in wafts of Estée Lauder and Chanel, but the highly polished floor, walls painted blue and cream, the perspectives of corridors, the glimpses of classrooms with their quiet rows of yellow desks made Hugo feel dizzyingly nostalgic for his own lost boyhood. Doors opened and shut again, nuns hurried with armfuls of glittering silks, rouged faces appeared and then suddenly withdrew giggling. A parent said, "Yes, she has a solo; the *tension*, my dear!" In his own schooldays he had been a highlight of the Dramatic Society and made a splendidly striding Viola with his clear voice and blond hair, and his Rosalind in high boots had produced some unexpected reactions afterwards among Brothers and older boys. But the thrill of it all, sweat and greasepaint backstage, stifled whispers, anxious producers, and yes, oh yes, that wicked thrill of silk skirts swishing round your thighs and ankles; of red lipstick pouting your mouth! Theatrical performances were responsible for some very odd shifts in affiliations; he'd fallen himself quite badly at seventeen, he remembered with embarrassment, for a provocative little Ariel, clad in nothing but a silver kilt.

The school hall was enormous, acres of parquet now covered by neat lines of stacking chairs fast filling up. Hugo's seat was near the front but at the end of a row — it was unlikely that Rachel gazing out over a sea of faces should recognise him there.

Lights were switched down and the darkness was punctuated by little dry coughs. Then a spotlight shone on a door by the stage through which a line of impeccably neat schoolgirls entered, clad in blue skirts, white shirts and ties of blue, gold and white (Mary's colours, what else?). A lay teacher sat down at the piano, the choir got into position and began to sing softly a version of Pergolesi's 'Salve Regina' with a throaty solo from a hefty young contralto. Hugo leaned back in his chair and decided he was going to enjoy himself. Slowly the heavy blue curtains parted;

behind was a greyish mist out of which a schoolgirl stepped and began to read from a scroll in elocuted tones: "The First Joyful Mystery: The Annunciation." Meanwhile, the choir started up again; this time Bach and *Ave Maria* and gradually the grey shapes behind the curtain were lit up.

In the centre of the stage stood a tall angel with arm aloft. Nearby knelt a young girl in a blue dress, hands crossed on her breast. Colours glowed, the composition was flawless. "*Isn't* she wonderful?" said the woman next to Hugo, who nodded agreement. The next Mystery was The Visitation. Barelegged children in striped tunics sat on the ground playing games, a woman balanced an urn on a hip, a blind beggar held out a hand, and in the middle the elderly veiled Elizabeth held out a hand to Rachel, her hair flowing as if she had just rushed there from a long distance away.

Later, black Philomena, racial pride evidently having been swallowed, knelt in a satin turban with a peacock feather, holding out a jewelled casket. A shepherd boy held a toy lamb. (A pity about the toy lamb. And about the plastic doll which was supposed to represent the Holy Child.) But it was at Rachel that everyone looked, radiant in her blue dress and white veil. It occurred to Hugo that she was probably the same age as the real Virgin would have been, and she certainly shared the same ethnic origins with her strong dark features, her thin arched nose, huge glowing eyes and mass of heavy hair.

Even the disbelievers had to admit that Sister Scholastica had made a good choice in Rachel Gold. And those who saw Sister Scholastica as she moved among her little production were impressed and surprised — her pale cheeks glowed pink and the smile that lit up her face showed her to be younger and prettier than they had realised. It was as though Rachel was producing miraculous transformations all round.

Mystery succeeded Mystery. The choir moved through Bach to Handel, and only some of the very youngest brothers and sisters grew restless in their seats. Finally, the Tableaux came to their climax; this one had been Sister Oliver Plunkett's favourite and was called 'Mary, the Mother of us all'. The choir, with their first lapse in taste, launched into the drone of the Lourdes hymn and the curtain swung back on a truly spectacular crowd scene. In front massed a group of Children of All Nations in which every black, brown, beige or yellow girl in the school had been brought in to do duty in a variety of national costumes. Poor Philomena was there in a grass skirt, her ample breasts concealed behind a not very ethnic bodice. A Chinese girl had been given a satin jacket and a pigtail. A pretty Indian wore a sari, a plump blonde had clogs and a Dutch bonnet. A child in Seven Sorrows uniform with an old-fashioned velour hat represented England. And in the centre of it all, high above them on a dais where blonde angels knelt and a single spotlight shone, stood Rachel, at this stage beginning to wobble ever so slightly. Her glorious hair was almost but not quite covered by a veil which reached down to her feet, there was a blue sash round her waist and a tumble of yellow roses (plastic, alas, the real ones being far too expensive at this time of the year) concealed her feet. For a while she stood there, hands outstretched and smiling. Hugo was overcome.

He was still overcome when he telephoned her. "Come to tea on Sunday," he said and then wondered, as he put the phone down, quite why he had asked her. The effect on Rachel at the other end of the line was indescribable. She trembled and shook so much that she had to go and light herself a cigarette in the hope that it would calm her down (it didn't). Yet that evening, the last of the three performances, she glowed with a quite startling radiance, which everybody noticed. "Was I all right, Sister?" she asked after the final curtain, and Sister Scholastica paused with her hand on her hip, and then broke into an unexpected smile. "Yes, Rachel," she said quietly, "you were all right."

Well, that was strange. Perhaps it was a sign that after all things were going to get better. Though her mother was still in a bad mood with her and making an excuse to get out of lunch at Grandmother's didn't help. "You just go your own sweet way, you never think about what difficulties you cause for the rest of us," she snapped. Not that Rachel had said anything about Hugo, of course. As far as her family knew, she was meeting Milly in the Tate Gallery.

It was a dismal afternoon; rain fell softly from a heavy saturated sky pocking the stirred grey surface of the water. The Thames curved away into a damp haze, through which domes and rooftops and towers quivered as if in a mirage, silvery and remote, barely anchored. Insubstantial Georgian houses fronted the river, and as she sat on the top of the 49 bus, she imagined herself grown up and sophisticated living in such a house, watching the rise and fall of the river, getting in and out of taxis with confidence, pushing open the plate glass doors of smart shops, being the owner of her life, and not as she felt now, an uncomfortable tenant somewhere on its fringes.

The bus stopped at the corner of the King's Road. She must walk down towards Peter Jones and take a turning — Hugo had given her careful instructions over the phone. She tried to make her mind a blank so that she would not arrive in a turmoil of dread, but it was so hard; the thoughts *would* intrude so that by the time she reached Sloane Square her palms were sweaty and there was a knot somewhere behind her breastbone. What did she look like? She had spent a long time on her appearance that afternoon, carefully assembling a whole outfit in her current favourite colours, using her new eyeshadow and a bright lipstick, and then suddenly catching sight of herself in her bedroom mirror, looking, she thought, like an overdecorated flagpole, had ripped everything off, putting on instead a plain grey skirt and her guernsey with only a smear of make-up. Now she saw what a fool she had been, the King's Road was full of such well-dressed people and she was to arrive at Hugo's like a frump! She hadn't read that poet he'd been on about either; he'd think she was an absolute moron.

Hugo's road was suddenly before her; tall houses curved in a sweep of rose and terracotta brick. Before she'd had time to think (or she would have turned and fled back home), she was standing on a doorstep of black and white marble, pressing the bell marked with his name. His voice came down through the intercom, distant and unfocused like the voice of God calling from the clouds.

It was dark in the hallway and the air was very still as though it had been undisturbed for a hundred years. Something prickled her nostrils; was it the smell of dust or the sweep of long-dead chambermaids' skirts brushing past? Heavy dark doors with a faint sheen to them were firmly shut with no sign that they would ever open or that life might go on inside them; the noise of the traffic outside was muffled. She climbed three flights of stairs; there was a smooth worn red carpet with old-fashioned brass stair rods. And then she heard him calling her in the stifled silence, "Come on up, Rachel, I'm on the top floor," and he was standing smiling at her in the doorway. He wore faded denims (though very clean, very pressed) and a pale blue sweater over an open-necked shirt. He looked, she thought, beautiful.

To her confusion he kissed her on the cheek, his face momentarily cool against hers, and said, "I expect you're cold," though clammy with nerves, she was not. "Come on in; I've banked the fire up."

The walls glowed soft pink and everywhere was the glitter of precious objects, china, gilt, glass. She had not imagined him living in such a flat, but now she had seen it, it was perfectly right. In the living room, a fire glowed brightly and he had made a cosy nest for himself on the hearthrug with cushions and piles of books. There was a tray, as well, with a pretty china pot and two cups. (Two, she saw with delight. So he had thought about her coming!) "Make yourself comfortable," he said, "while I put the kettle on." But where? She looked around in panic. On the sofa? The chair? It seemed presumptuous to sit on the floor, so she pretended to study the objects on the mantelpiece. "Isn't it lovely," he said, suddenly coming behind her, "it's William de Morgan. I've been having a very pleasant afternoon," he went on, "with some old friends," and she was taken aback until she realised that the old friends he meant were books. "I've been reading Crashaw on Saint Teresa; a marvellous poem. Do you know it?" She shook her head. "Then I must read you a bit. Let's have some tea. I hope you like Lapsang Souchong." The unfamiliar names swirled through her head: Lapsang Souchong sounded like a poet and Crashaw sounded like a tea, it was all very confusing. Still, when he had put the teapot down, he sat on the floor, so it seemed only natural to join him there, looking at the flames. "I thought we'd make some toast," he went on, "since I've got this nice fire. Do you want to take a turn with the toasting fork, or shall I?" She said she would since she was too nervous to be unoccupied and leaned towards the blaze as if it would absorb some of the heat she felt suffusing her cheeks while the fragrance of the strange tea filled the air beside her.

"How is your book going?" she asked.

"Oh," he said, "rather well, actually," and started to tell her. She could not follow it all, but it was nice just to listen to his voice. Then he told her about his attempt to interview Anne Marie and how unrewarding it had been. She managed to burn a piece of toast. "Do you . . ." She wanted to say "Do you believe in visions?" but it seemed too personal and direct, so instead she said, "Do you find it difficult to write?" and the conversation drifted as he told her about his routine at the typewriter. It seemed that he *did* find it difficult to write, most awfully, and yet if that were true, he would hardly be sitting there smiling about it, would he? Moreover, Anne Marie Kelly had somehow taken a stand between them, squat, dumpy and unsmiling. God, how fed up she was with Anne Marie and all her silly stories!

"Do you suppose . . ." she began as another piece of toast turned brown before the glowing coals.

"Cinnamon sugar, or gentleman's relish?" he interrupted her.

"I've never had gentleman's relish; it sounds very . . . very . . ." How she longed to insert some clever literary comparison such as he would surely have done but she was unable to think of anything, so she tailed off feebly ". . . cinnamon sugar, please."

"Rachel," said Hugo, as he spooned cinnamon on to her toast. "I have a confession to make. No, don't look so startled. I came to see you the other day in your Tableaux."

"Oh no!" she said and in her horror dropped a piece of bread right into the fire, where it flamed up.

"They were very good. And you looked marvellous."

"I wish you hadn't come," she said. "I hated doing it. But there's this nun who bullies me."

"I'm glad she bullied you. No one else would have done it so nicely."

"Well, it's all over now. I shan't have to do it again."

"I had a very pleasant evening. And I managed to have a good look round the convent without their knowing, since your Reverend Mother won't give me an interview. I felt quite pleased with myself."

"It's a prison," she said with vehemence.

"It's certainly a very gloomy building."

"Not just that. It's . . . you can't get away. You can't even have your thoughts to yourself. They're there all the time listening. And if you're not a Catholic, it's even worse. Like a game where you don't know the words or the rules but you have to join in. I'm sorry. I'm moaning about myself. I didn't mean to. What about that poem you were going to tell me about?"

"'Love thou art absolute sole Lord, of life and death. . . .' Yes, it's wonderful. I want to use it in the introduction to my book but I don't quite know how to work it in. But it seems to me to be so absolutely central, that is, if you're examining something like this. There. I'm sorry. Now I'm going on about myself."

"No, I like it when you do. Please."

"Well, you see, it seems to me that at the heart of any true vision there has to be love. Overwhelming. Without it, there's no truth and a vision is just hysterical fantasy. It's as though the power of the visionary's love summons down God, who's normally very reluctant to commit himself, and forces him to react. You see, unless we generate it, God's love is switched off."

Rachel tried to understand what he meant. When Hugo talked about God and love it sounded very different from when Sister Imelda spoke of the same things. In Sister Imelda's mouth both God and love sounded forbidding, as though they were made of some very heavy iron and it was an effort to lift them. But when she thought of love it was something quite different again. She turned to look at Hugo, his clear features outlined in firelight, silvery fair hair falling over his face. When she thought of love, there was nothing of God in it.

"Listen," he said, opening a book. "All about love and death, and the double meanings those words can have. And the underlying meaning which is about God.

> . . . she never undertook to know
> What Death with love should have to do,
> Nor hath she 'ere yet understood
> Why to shew love, she should shed blood. . . ."

Rachel did not understand either, and yet it did not matter, for his words seemed to be taking effect on her at quite a different level. It was rather like that time at Paul's party where she'd drunk too much vodka and she'd seemed to float away to somewhere else, where a whole different set of values operated. As she sat by the fire, Hugo talked on and on. He seemed too engrossed with his theory which was something to do with the strength of emotions to worry about whether she understood what he was going on about, but that didn't worry her as the sound of his voice and the flickering of the firelight lulled her. It was enough, just to be there, in that marvellous room.

She pushed aside the tea tray and leaned back against the edge of the sofa.

"You see," he went on, "the divine and the human meet at only one moment and that's love. God needs love, as we do. That's what they mean when they talk of man being made in God's image. Without love, man is a machine and God's an abstraction. With love, man shares in the divine nature. It's as simple as that."

To Rachel, it seemed as simple as quantum physics. She thought the only question was whether to believe in God or not. Some mornings she did, some mornings she didn't.

"Am I boring you, Rachel?" he said. But without waiting for an answer, he went on talking and then abstractedly slid an arm around her shoulder. She tensed and trembled.

"At school," she said, to try and steady herself, "they tell us that the Song of Solomon is Christ's song to the Church. But it doesn't sound at all like that to me."

"Oh, the Song of Solomon!" he cried enthusiastically. "And how it's embarrassed the Church! But no, I don't think it's a problem. If, as I believe, earthly love is simply a metaphor for divine, then there's no distinction. Christ loves and man loves. How or why doesn't matter, as long as the love's there. Isn't it wonderful stuff! 'Thy lips are as a thread of scarlet. . . .'" She didn't realise for a few moments because the tone of his voice was unchanged that he was quoting.

"'. . . and thy speech is comely, thy temples are as a piece of pomegranate within thy locks.' Isn't that beautiful? Pomegranate — can you imagine opening a pomegranate and seeing the seeds there like jewels? I always think of poor Persephone too, and that piece of pomegranate which condemned her to a living death."

Her head had begun to whirl with allusion and quotation. It began to whirl even more when she found that he, still in that half-abstracted way, was kissing her on the mouth. And then he broke away again and carried on with the quotation: "'Thou art beautiful, O my love, comely as Jerusalem, terrible as an army with banners! Turn away thine eyes from me, for they have overcome me. . . .' Rachel," he added suddenly. "Oh, Rachel."

His mouth was cool, scented still with tea; but he did not seem so abstracted now as he bent over her and began kissing her with urgency. She felt herself being swept away, away, there was no time to think or reason or worry, just the overwhelming flood of her feelings and his actions. She had often wondered what it would be like, but now there was no space for wondering. "'My beloved is mine and I am his,'" she thought, for she knew the words too. "'He feedeth among the lilies. . . .'"

Chapter 17

"I must go," said Rachel much later and she picked up her clothes. Hugo was half-asleep, but he got up and went to the door of his flat with her, wrapped in a bathrobe. "I must go," she said again, a little wistfully, as though she wanted to be asked to stay; but he said, "It would have been lovely if you could have stayed," and kissed her. "Lovely Rachel," he said, as he opened the door for her.

Left alone, he wandered back into his living room and sank down before the embers of the fire. His thoughts at this moment were all confused. *Post coitum*. . . . Was it just that? That the small death he had just known had left behind it a small bereavement? He shivered and reached for his clothes; there was almost no heat left in the fire now.

For the rest of the evening, he mooched around the flat, depleted of energy. All he could think of was Rachel's slender pale body and what they had done together. Impossible to work, impossible to read the Dostoevsky he had set aside for that evening. Why had it all been so much more draining than Antonia's joyous sexual Olympics ever were?

The next morning he had planned to go to Victoria and the Catholic library just behind the cathedral. He caught the bus at Knightsbridge and took a seat upstairs. Leaning back, he found his mind being filled with images of Rachel. He remembered her sitting by the fire, outlined in flame, and how they had made love. As he thought about it, he began to feel soft and voluptuous, as boneless as a rag doll. The vague feelings washed through and through him and began to be less vague. He felt the beginnings of an erection and quickly pulled himself upright, covering his lap with his plastic file.

As he sat there, a group of louts came up the stairs and threw themselves across several seats behind him. The bus lurched forward and then stopped, caught in a worse than usual jam at Hyde Park Corner. The loudest and most loutish of the louts started up a monologue that no one in the bus could ignore, nor were they intended to.

"'Always on Top'" he read, quoting from an advertisement. "That's me, eh, Gav, always on top, eh Gav, just give me the chance, right, that little fat one at the party, ooh she wuz a right goer wunt she Gav, ooh stop it you, she goes, but I din stop it did I Gav, did I Tel, eh, did I, you dirty bugger, he's as bad as I am, inne, yes you are, bad as I am, go on, own up, never stop thinking about it, do you, bad as I am, go on, you are, you're a dirty bugger, Tel, just wait till I tell your mum how you and that Julie carried on in yerolidays, at it like fuckin bunny rabbits, they were, mind, I can't complain, can I , what was her name, Tracy, dirty cow, once she seen what I got, couldn't get enough of it, could she. . . ."

And so on. The chaste lawns and shrubberies of Buckingham Palace witnessed his unending accounts and old ladies turned round in disapproval. Hugo too was compelled to listen, and found his own pleasant eroticism transformed to something different and unclean. How had he been any different from the youth in the bus, seducing a schoolgirl like that? People like himself wrapped things up in fancy language, but in the end they came down to the same thing. He'd been a dirty bugger and she was a right little goer. By the time he got off the bus at the terminal, he felt dirty all right.

Instead of going straight to the library, he went to the cathedral, hoping those cool dark spaces would quench the inflammation of body and soul. What had he done to Rachel? A man of nearly thirty, he'd let himself be carried away like any randy lout; a schoolgirl of seventeen! Dirty bugger, dirty bugger.

Oh, Antonia, he thought, why did you go away and leave me at the mercy of my instincts? For with Antonia, there was no guilt. Everything was different with Antonia.

In the chapels, little patches of mosaic glowed dark gold. Once he had been here with an old Catholic aunt when he was a child. She had told him how costly the mosaics were; that one day they would cover the whole interior, but first the money must be raised. Entranced, he had put sixpence in the collecting drum and dreamed of the day when he would return to see the glittering crust of gold transforming the dark red brick everywhere. His soul had thrilled with the mystery.

Mysteries, mysteries. Once the world so full of them, plump apples in a basket, just out of reach, and the thought of the day when in a blinding flash of realisation all would be his.

But now, as he looked at the gloomy deep crimson heights of the cathedral, where pallid shafts of light barely pierced the gloom, and the dark gleam, here and there, of gold, he knew that this was where the mystery lay; in the unfinished cathedral. The promise of those glittering patches was more exciting than its fulfilment could ever be. The mysteries of his childhood had turned out after all to be prosaic and disappointing; they were not mysteries at all. Completed, the cathedral would be no more than a brash, gaudy palace.

He should not have slept with Rachel.

Coming out of the cathedral, a smiling woman handed him a pamphlet. He stuffed it into his pocket without noticing. But later when he sat in the library, he spread it out on the table and looked at it.

THE VIRGIN OF THE COMMON! WHAT HAS SHE TO SAY TO US?
In these troubled times, people look for enlightenment and too often there seems to be none there! That is why Our Lady has chosen to appear to us, as she has appeared many many times before to her erring children, urging them to Repent before it is Too Late! It was the THIRD SECRET of Fatima revealed by the Bishop of Leira in 1960 that urged World leaders KRUSHCHEV, KENNEDY and MACMILLAN to sign the Test-Ban treaty in 1960, the secret that was TOO TERRIFYING for the rest of the world!

Now the world is in urgent need again, and once more Our Lady has chosen to reveal her message through a Simple Child! This time, let us Heed it; Soon it May be Too Late!!

If you are interested, please write to us S.A.V.E. (The Society for the Apparitions of the Virgin in England) at the following address. . . .

Mysteries, mysteries. A girl on a South London common, and an unfinished building. Was that, in the end, all they were? Was the simple message that there were no mysteries any more?

Rachel's appearance in school that Monday caused some comment. "What a pretty creature that little Jewish girl is," said Sister Walpurgis. Everyone felt that Sister Scholastica's rather unusual choice had been triumphantly justified. The Tableaux had been an outstanding success. Everybody felt it and success filled the school with a cloud of euphoria; they had to talk about it, the sets, the singing, the costumes. And Rachel.

"So pretty. Just like that lovely painting — is it Raphael?"

"And so dignified and natural. What a pity that girl isn't a Catholic."

"Yes, she'd make such a good Catholic, that one, I think."

"Jews who convert make *very* good Catholics," said Sister Aloysius. "Does anybody remember old Sister Michael from Aylesbury? Now *she* was Jewish, and . . ."

"Here's Sister Schol. Well done, Sister Schol. We've all been talking about your triumph."

"Yes, it was a triumph, wasn't it?" said Sister Scholastica. She seemed a changed person today, smiling and full of charm, so that you felt that after all there was a real woman inside the shell. But there was also, you might have noticed too (Sister Mark did, though she put it down to the excitement of the Tableaux), something febrile and slightly dangerous in the charm.

"And how clever of you to think of your Rachel. We didn't agree at first, but you were right."

"Of course I was right. I knew we could do it."

They still wanted to talk about Rachel. "The family is quite well off, isn't it?"

"You know these Jewish professional families. They know how to look after themselves. They work hard too, I'll say that. Rachel is a very good little worker."

"Of course she is," said Sister Scholastica, still smiling. "Rachel can succeed at anything she puts her mind to. That's why I think . . ."

"What do you think, Sister?" For Sister Scholastica's words had trailed off and she stared dreamily into the air.

"Why," she said still softly, "that girl is made for God. Rachel Gold will become a nun. God has marked her out."

This was greeted with a murmur of surprise. Nobody had ever heard Sister Scholastica talk about God like this before.

"But Sister, aren't you . . ."

"Aren't I what?" said Sister smiling pleasantly. "Oh I'm sure of it, my dear Sisters. Rachel may not know it yet, but you can't escape when God has his hand on you. Rachel will be a nun."

Rachel's own euphoria lasted well into Tuesday. But by the evening a small edge of doubt had inserted itself. It had been so wonderful. She longed to see him again, to touch him. And it must, so strong a feeling, mustn't it, be shared? It couldn't be otherwise. Could it?

But in the post that Tuesday morning, a letter arrived for Hugo. Now it lay on his desk, where he had read it he didn't know how many times.

> Darling Hugo,
> It's no good, Charles is a brute and a bore and I can't stand him. I can't stand you either, but it's different. I want to marry you and you have to say yes or no soon. If you say no I shall never see you again. Doesn't that sound melodramatic? But it's no use, I can't get you out of my system. Anyway, I'm tired of being an old maid, and so should you be. I want babies and a

house and lots and lots of lovely sex with you. I don't even mind you going to church every Sunday. Think about it, darling. I'm sure it'd do you good to be married, and I would look after you. Oh, and by the way, I don't know if it'll influence you but I've already got the house. Aunt Mim has just died and left me that dear little house in Glebe Place. Hugo, do say yes, you bastard. I'll phone Wednesday.

    With bated breath
    (What *does* that mean do you know?)
    Antonia

Reverend Mother had had a letter too, but hers did not make her feel happy.

'As you know,' it read, 'the policy of the Church in recent years has been to modernise wherever possible and in our urban multi-ethnic diocese, we have found that we cannot ignore the demands of the twentieth century. Funds and morale are low — certain projects, for example, a crèche for working mothers in Brixton, a hostel for young drug addicts, are urgently needed and we feel it particularly important that such things are part of the Church's umbrella of care. We know that the Seven Sorrows has done many years of faithful service and produced generations of good Catholic young women, but we feel now that in this day and age the cost of maintaining such an institution is beyond us. We are not, of course, talking about an immediate closure, but a period of, say, two years could be allowed to ensure that the merger with the Sacred Heart is as smooth as possible. . . .'

At the side of her desk, a chubby little Hummel figure grinned coyly at her. She brought her fist down hard so that it trembled in surprise.

Chapter 18

The Apparition that week brought the biggest crowd ever. Several thousand believers turned up; the cynics were there too but less in evidence. The inspector in charge of the large police operation said he had never known such a well-behaved crowd; it was a pleasure to turn out his men. Those who had thought of setting up mobile shops selling holy souvenirs were doing a bomb, and a fibreglass model of the Virgin of the Common as described by Anne Marie and turned out in its thousands had already saved a small mouldings factory in Tooting Bec from closure. Television cameras were there to record every moment of the scene at close hand, so that it was possible for everyone in the country to be their own judge of her sincerity. And indeed, as the image of the rapt, sublimely unconscious small face filled the multiplied screens of the nation, it was hard to feel totally cynical. Fame and attention had subtly changed her; she had fined down and glowed so that the brimming enigmatic green eyes were now more prominent, she moved with more grace, more confidence, and her little figure with arms stretched out before the invisible image had become one of the most familiar pictures in the country.

Our Lady's message was simple, and direct. There must be repentance; there would be a church. There was a secret for Anne Marie which she was not to tell for many years, soon God would reveal Himself. Anne Marie had now developed a mannerism of repeating the Virgin's statements as they were uttered, and so millions heard this on live television. At that point a strange thing happened and in spite of the huge crowds that were there, there was very little agreement on what it was. As Anne Marie spoke to

Our Lady, it seemed to some people that the soft dense rain had stopped, the clouds parted and a strange light seemed to be shed everywhere. Some said it was a pinkish light, some a yellowish. Some could see nothing at all. And then the moon, which should not have risen for some time, could clearly be seen, gleaming like a flat disc of polished silver. Some people said it seemed to sway from side to side, some said it slowly expanded. Later when videos were played back, there was nothing to be seen except a whitish patch in the sky. Tomorrow all these stories would be thrown into the cauldron from which legends emerge. More than one person would claim that the silvery shape had zig-zagged across the sky, but this may have been wishful thinking, in imitation of the spinning sun of Fatima. It was all a little confusing, but perhaps there should always be an air of ambiguity about a miracle, so that God does not deprive the unbeliever of his right to unbelief.

Rachel did not give Anne Marie a thought that next Saturday. Her mind, with a mixture of tenderness and anxiety, was all on Hugo. She decided to make an excuse to go to Chelsea and ring his doorbell. If he were not in, she would come home again. But if he were . . . oh, it would be wonderful!

As she walked to the bus stop, she knew she must take him a gift. But what would serve? It was in a greengrocer's shop that she saw the answer. Pomegranates. Certainly they had lost something in the journey between Solomon's garden and South London, but they were still oddly beautiful with their thick skins that bloomed with scarlet and honey yellow under a patina of silver-gilt. She bought a dozen; they were heavy and expensive. The greengrocer tipped them into a plastic bag, and she cradled the bag as she sat, dazed and dreaming, on the top of the bus to Chelsea.

Hugo, wheeling his trolley through the glittering stacks, planned the meal. He had already bought smoked salmon, not really very subtle, but she adored it so why not? There was to be something a little *nouvelle* for afterwards, wisps of chicken breasts on a purée of artichoke hearts for example, with a salad of kiwi fruit, followed by a tart of apricots marinaded in amoretto liqueur, and a little *fromage de chèvre*. . . .

Lady Bathmaker's overloud voice broke into his thoughts. "Dear Mr Swann, how very pleasant to see you. Do you think you could reach me down a packet of those tea bags? I believe they imagine one is a giant." He obliged and she went on, "Although I do *adore* this shop, don't you? Bring back the little corner grocer, some say, but I remember those places and they were terrible! Obsequious little men and no choice at all. I'm a fearfully *supermarket* person myself. Do you know their smoked mackerel pâté? My *dear*, let me recommend it to you."

"Do let me rest your basket on my trolley," he said, looking at the uncertain grip of her knotted fingers and cursing the necessity of gentlemanly conduct. Shoppers turned to look as they passed. Really, she might be addressing the Albert Hall; if only she would get her hearing aid adjusted!

"I suppose you too had one of those letters from our dear landlord," she went on. "Isn't it a shame? I expect they'll double the rent and fill the place full of Arabs, though even Arabs, they say, can't afford us these days. I shall go and live with my sister in Wiltshire, you know. We don't get on at all, and I'm sure we shall be thoroughly miserable, but there you are, old age is *such* a bore. I'd grown quite fond of my little flat."

"So had I," said Hugo.

"By the way," she continued, "I saw the most *devastatingly* pretty girl coming out of your flat the other day. My dear! What a lucky young man you are! So many pretty girls!"

"Not really so many, I hope," said Hugo dubiously.

"Exactly!" exclaimed Lady Bathmaker, who of course had misheard him. "Gather ye rosebuds and all that. And the girls *are* so pretty these days aren't they? I don't blame you one little bit."

"But I don't exactly . . ."

"After all," she said, ignoring him, "one day you'll be as ancient as I am, and then, my dear, there's nothing left but memories, so it's wise to ensure that they're nice ones, isn't it?"

"Yes, but . . ."

But her voice had risen to a resonant crescendo, and several curious shoppers turned to look as she bestowed the culmination of her thought process on Hugo.

"If a young man doesn't have *dozens* of mistresses then there must be something wrong with him, mustn't there? No my dear, you keep it up. Just you keep it up!"

Anne Marie did not get out on her own much now but today she had. Mr Blackaby had taken the rest of the family to Woburn Abbey for the day, but she said she had a headache and they let her stay behind.

It was very dark in the church and a little cold. It was funny being there when it was all empty, she thought; it was a bit spooky. Would Father come, or would she have to find him? She thought he would come soon.

Perhaps they made it like this on purpose to frighten you. Whenever she came for Saturday evening confession she always had this funny picture of everyone sitting there with their sins perching on their shoulders like big ugly black birds. For sins were ugly, everyone said so, they darkened everywhere with their nasty wings, they stuck their claws into you. But what she'd never been able to imagine was what happened to those big black birds when you went into confession. Afterwards your sins left you as clean as if they'd never been there, so what happened to them, then? Where did they go? Did they go to the priest? Did they sit on his shoulder instead? It must be uncomfortable for him sitting there at the end of the day crouched beneath all that black ugly clamouring weight. It didn't do to think about it. Anne Marie had always been good at not thinking about things. Otherwise she might see her dad, lying there in the loony bin, twitching. Poor dad! He'd been such a big lovely man too, he used to swing her up on to his shoulder and throw her into the air. And the only reason he'd gone to the site that day had been to show her off to his mates, for it was his day off. His little flower, he called her. If he hadn't gone then the thing wouldn't have fallen on his head and done all that damage.

But you couldn't think about that, either.

If the priest didn't come soon, she might change her mind and go home, so there. Of course she'd never meant . . . she hadn't known Mum would make it so hard to stop, but it had all been such fun, hadn't it? Mum was talking about getting married to Mr Blackaby and going to live in New Zealand. They'd have a big fridge and a video and everything. So it would be best really if she got that black bird out of the way first. The priest wouldn't tell anyone, she knew that. She wouldn't get into any trouble.

Ooh, here he was, coming through the sacristy door. Hallo! She'd wave at him. He was quite nice, Father Joyce, even though her mum didn't like him. Once he'd given her chocolate at Christmas.

"Why, Anne Marie!" he said. "What are you doing here?"

"I want to go to confession, Father."

"But confessions don't start till six."

"I know," she said, "but it doesn't matter. You can do it any old time, can't you?"

He looked at her with the beginnings of panic. No, he didn't want that big black bird any more than she did. "Anne Marie, if you have something to talk about why don't we go and sit in my house? It's much more comfortable there."

"No." she said. That wouldn't do, of course. "I want to stay here."

"Then talk away, Anne Marie. I'm listening."

Oh no, he wasn't getting her like that. "I want proper confession. Can we go into the box, please?"

And Father Joyce, looking at her with a sinking heart and fearing what she was going to confess, had no choice but to agree.

Chapter 19

The downstairs door had been left open and so she went straight up, hoping she wouldn't bump into that mad old lady as she had done coming down last time. When she rang Hugo's doorbell, there was such a long pause that she thought he must be out and had almost begun to register a sort of relief when she saw his shadowy shape slowly materialise behind the glass door.

The door opened and he stood there. He was wearing a huge apron and the sleeves of his white shirt were rolled up above the elbow. "Why . . ." he began to say. For a moment the ghost of a welcoming smile hung on his face and then it faded. She realised in a dreadful instant that she had been on the receiving end of a welcome intended for somebody else. "Rachel . . . you'd better come in."

Still clutching her carrier bag, she followed him. The little room now glowed its welcome for another; the dining table laid with two sets of cutlery, two glasses, two linen napkins.

"Oh, er, that," he said. He seemed almost as nervous as she was. "I've got an . . . an old school friend coming. Look, do sit down." And he showed her towards the place where only a week before. . . . But strangely she felt nothing now, only a horrible numbness. "Er, can I get you some tea?"

"Lapsang Souchong?" she said with a half smile, which he did not return.

"How about tea?" he repeated, having by now got some control of himself and managing a note of heartiness.

But tea would always be a lover's drink for Rachel now. "No, thank you."

He sat down opposite her, first having taken off that ridiculous apron. A swathe of fair hair fell over his forehead. "Look, Rachel . . ." he said. "The thing is. . . . Oh God, I'm making an awful mess of this."

She did not try to help him out.

"You see, last Saturday . . . it was a wonderful experience."

"Sunday."

"Sunday, then. What happened . . ." He looked up at her for a moment with eyes that seemed momentarily to light up at the memory. "It was wonderful, Rachel. It was something very beautiful. For both of us, I hope. Certainly for me . . ."

"But," she said coldly, hearing it in his voice.

"Look, it's just that. . . . It's not that I don't respect you, Rachel. I do, most awfully. I should hate you to think I was one of those types."

"You've just gone off me, is that it?"

"Oh no." He sounded genuinely shocked. "Goodness me, no. You're . . . you're a very special person, Rachel, make no mistake about that. One day, you'll . . . oh no, please don't ever knock yourself; you're something quite . . ."

There was a long silence. He looked down at his hands, as though they might contain the answer. All the excuses flashed before his eyes. Antonia, his engagement, his religion, the louts on the bus and his resolve not to give way to baser instincts. But it was no good. They simply would not wear, any of them. In the end, he simply held out his hands and looked up at her through the sweep of his hair, haunted and hurt. "I'm sorry." To Rachel he had never looked more beautiful.

"*Are* you? Are you really?" But there seemed no point in prolonging the conversation.

As she stepped out into the row of terracotta houses, Rachel realised that she still had the bag of pomegranates in her hand. *I opened to my beloved, but my beloved had withdrawn himself and gone; my soul failed when he spake. . . .*

She clutched it tightly in her hand and then threw it into the nearest rubbish bin.

★

There were to be no more visions, announced Anne Marie that evening. No, Our Lady had not appeared to tell her so, but instead she had received one of those inner messages which the faithful called 'locutions' to say that Our Lady had delivered her message and the rest was up to mankind. But Anne Marie, to whom elaboration had now become second nature, added that she had promised 'great blessings' to all those who were faithful in her cult.

Still, there were people to be found on the common most evenings, just in case. Naturally the council still procrastinated on the subject of a shrine, but a permanent display of sorts was usually to be found and of recent weeks had been left alone. Those whom Our Lady had blessed had stuck little wooden crosses in the ground with pencilled messages of thanks, and there were flowers in milk bottles and plastic containers.

When it was dark and the last pious stranger had gone home, Bonko the skinhead, who had been hanging around all day, sidled into the area. His little sister had just gone into hospital. Silently, savagely, he set about ripping out all the little crosses, upsetting the milk bottles, stamping on the flowers.

"Some more of Mrs Mottram's wonderful trifle?" said the Bishop to Father Grant, who was the senior priest of the diocese. It was always good to talk things over with Father Grant, whom he had known since their seminary days.

"Delicious!" said Father Grant.

"She's done us proud tonight," said the Bishop.

"Indeed she has! Do convey my thanks."

"Did I tell you that the Holy Father's message came today?"

"Really! What did he say?"

"More or less to reiterate what we've already concluded. That the impact on the church has been so positive that we don't want it to seem that we're being overly grudging and sceptical. Of course, we don't want to go overboard with the old credulity, but for the moment . . ."

"A little tactical fence-sitting? I say, could I have that last cherry?"

"There's quite a cult already in Italy, you know. They've taken our young Bernadette to their hearts. Apparently Mrs K. did an interview on Italian television that went down very well."

"Perhaps we can begin to do a little local encouragement. By the way, any news about poor Father Joyce?"

"Nothing new, I'm afraid. I did phone the other day and had a word. For some reason everything got on top of him and he needs a complete break. He sounded quite unlike his old self."

"Still, the nuns there are very good, aren't they?"

"Marvellous. And of course very experienced at dealing with this sort of thing. I'm afraid there's quite a lot of it among our priests at the moment, more than people realise."

"Well, you know my views on that," said Father Grant. "I put it all down to the pressures of celibacy."

"And you know my views too. It might sound old-fashioned, but if we're meant to have the strength then God will give it to us."

"Still, bad luck on Father Joyce. I didn't know him that well, but he seemed a decent enough chap."

"Oh yes. Still is for all I know. Salt of the earth and all that."

Father Grant popped the cherry into his mouth with a roguish look. "But drear," he said. "Awfully drear."

The Bishop smiled back. "Yes. Oh my word yes."

On the Wednesday of that week, Hugo decided to go and visit his mother, who had been nagging him for some time to help her prune the roses. She lived in an unpractical chocolate-box cottage, a warren of tiny asymmetrical rooms and low beams; Hugo was continually knocking himself out as he negotiated low doorways and sloping floors. A wild garden charged and clambered round the house, jasmine, clematis, honeysuckle, roses. Hugo struggled with the secateurs and his thoughts at the same time. "Do be careful," said his mother. "You can give yourself very nasty blood poisoning from roses."

"I *know*." Being offered advice by someone who had no intention of helping always made him ratty. She laughed her light little laugh. "What a bad mood you're in today."

"I'm not. As it happens I'm in a very good mood. You just bring out the worst in me."

"Mothers always do that to people." She sighed. "I don't know why that should be, do you? You said on the phone you had some news for me."

"Ah, yes. What about this big branch, does it stay or does it go, do you think?"

"Oh, get rid of it. Hugo . . ."

"If you were to treat yourself to some decent gardening gloves, I wouldn't get scratched to ribbons."

"Hugo, you are prevaricating. What about this news?"

"Ah yes. Well, Mother, the thing is, I'm thinking about getting married."

"Hugo!" With a melodramatic gasp she dropped the trug she had been carrying. Plastic flower pots rolled away. He gave an embarrassed little laugh. "Well, that was certainly a response all right. I only said *thinking*."

"But my darling boy, thinking is further than you've ever got on the subject before. You know I had really begun to think you might be homosexual after all."

"You seem quite obsessed with this. You're obviously determined to be the mother of a homosexual, aren't you?"

"Hugo, you're being very unfair. I don't think you realise how much I worry. One day you'll be a parent yourself and then you'll know what it's like."

"Well, in the natural course of events I probably will be now, won't I? Don't you even want to know who it is?"

"I imagine it's probably that Amanda, isn't it?"

"If she's going to be your daughter-in-law you might at least get her name right. You know perfectly well she's Antonia."

"You've had such a quick turnover I can't keep up. I'm sure there was an Amanda once. How does Antonia feel about having me for a mother-in-law?"

"Since she's hardly had time to get used to the thought of having me for a husband, I shouldn't imagine it has even crossed her mind."

"Then it should do. Supposing we don't get on."

"Mother, are you doing this on purpose? You're supposed to say well done, congratulations, something like that."

"Well of course all those things. You know that. But this is so . . . sudden. Married. You."

"Married," he said. "Me." Put that way it did sound rather final. "As I said, we're thinking about it."

"She won't let go of you now she's got you this far. Women are like that you know. She's got you all right."

"I'm quite happy to be got, thank you."

She gave him a look. "Quite happy. But not passionately in love, I'd say."

"Passionately! Mother you're talking like a schoolgirl. This is nearly the twenty-first century, and people don't live lives written by Mills and Boon. Antonia and I . . ."

"Yes? Go on."

"Are very fond . . ."

"Come now, dear, that isn't enough. *Very fond* isn't going to carry you through forty years of dandruff and constipation. You have to do better than very fond."

"Then if you insist, we *love* each other. All right?"

"I hope so, Hugo. I really do hope so."

Chapter 20

If happiness showed in Rachel's face as beauty then unhappiness did the reverse. In fact so much so that when she went back to school on Monday, many of the nuns and teachers wondered why they had always thought her such a pretty girl; her skin was sallow and waxen, there were dark crescents under her eyes, her nose had a beaky look. "I'd never noticed before how fearfully *Jewish* the girl looks," said Sister Walpurgis with a note of distaste.

At the end of the morning, she had a Greek lesson with Sister Scholastica in the needlework room. She was Sister's only A-level student and they were alone beneath a statue of Saint Anne.

"'Having said these things . . .'" stammered Rachel, "'Athene of the . . . of the . . .'"

"'Bright'," interpolated Sister. She looked at Rachel curiously.

"'Bright eyes . . . went back to Olympus, where men say the Gods have . . . made their home for ever . . . their everlasting home. Touched' . . . no . . ."

"'Shaken.' Rachel, what is the matter with you today?"

"I'm sorry, Sister. I'm — I'm not feeling very well."

"I can see that," said Sister. Her voice was unusually soft and gentle. Rachel barely noticed it. She tried to turn her attention to Athene again. "'Shaken by no storms . . . not wet . . . not soaked by rain, not touched by snow . . .'"

"This is not a difficult passage," said Sister. "You should be able to translate it without any trouble. Did you prepare it last night?"

"No," said Rachel. "That is . . ."

These last few days Sister felt curiously light-headed. She kept forgetting things, but knew that the things she forgot were not important; she had smiled a lot and been charming to Sister Mark.

Now she knew that there was something to say to Rachel and that here was the time to say it.

She closed her *Odyssey*.

"Rachel?"

"Yes, Sister?" Rachel, a thousand miles away in a cold icebound kingdom, barely noticed the change in her teacher. Her only aim was to get through this day, as she would have to get through all the others which lay ahead.

"Your performance as Our Lady, Rachel. It was splendid."

"What? Oh, thank you, Sister."

"But today, I can see, you have something on your mind. Would you like to tell me about it?" Rachel started up in horror. "You can tell me, you know. Nuns can hear anything, did you know that? You can say anything to me."

Tell Sister? Tell a *nun*? Oh, God, not in a million years. *Sister*?

But Sister carried on: "These crises of the soul, Rachel, these dark nights, are a sign of God's special love. When He loves someone especially He sends a crisis to test that person. . . ."

Rachel heard her through a mist. She stared up at Sister, uncomprehending, her dark eyes tragic. Sister took her silence as a token of complicity.

". . . and I think He has sent me to be the one to . . . Rachel, there is an understanding between us, isn't there?"

The mist began to clear. Suddenly Rachel realised that she was in the middle of a peculiar situation. Sister's eyes were unnaturally bright, and as she spoke, she moved and nodded her head in a strange manner.

"Become a Catholic, Rachel," she whispered, leaning closer. "Become a Catholic. It is the only way." Her glittering eyes came closer and closer to Rachel. Aflame with a cold fire, now there was something almost beautiful about her. Little tendrils of hair escaped from her veil. Pink spots burned in her cheeks. "Become a Catholic. You are one of God's chosen. He wants you, Rachel. He wants you all for Himself. You are one of us, Rachel. You are one of the Beloved Ones. . . ."

And then Sister did something that all her instincts, all her years of training, should have told against: she reached out and stroked Rachel softly, first the cloud of her hair, down, down to Rachel's shoulder. In that second, Rachel, who had been mesmerised, came to her senses. Recoiling from Sister's touch as though a snake had bitten her, she jumped to her feet. The *Odyssey* and a sheaf of file paper slithered to the floor.

"For heaven's sake!" she cried, in a voice that came out curiously small and ineffectual.

"For heaven's sake," said Sister, still smiling. "For God's sake. For *my* sake, Rachel. . . ."

Rachel stood opposite the nun, who was sitting at the table, her pale hand extended as though it still felt the touch of Rachel's hair.

"God loves you so much, Rachel, you can see that, can't you? He loves you so much, He would die for you. Did die for you. He loves you so much, you see. . . ."

This was so unlike anything Rachel had ever expected or encountered before that she was quite bereft of words. Sister went on talking. She talked of God, and Love. She seemed to say the same thing many times over. She talked of being a nun, of giving yourself to God as to a lover. She spoke of love sweeping one away on a great flood. For Rachel it was as though a mouldering grave had been opened before her.

Still Sister smiled and talked. Eventually, Rachel left her there and ran from the needlework room. The first nun she saw was Sister Louis. "I think you'd better go and have a look at Sister Scholastica," she said.

Father Joyce stared at the red bars of electric heater that filled the space where a fire might have been. The nuns had just brought him a cup of coffee but he did not particularly want to drink it.

Things went round and round in his head, came back to where they started, and then began again, round and round. He was in a position from which he could not move.

The point was, it was simply impossible not to believe in God. The concept had worked its way right into the depths of his being; it would not be dislodged now.

So what you were left with was not the option of atheism, which would have freed you in other directions; but with the prospect of a God who existed all right, but who simply was not very kind. A God who took a malicious pleasure in playing nasty tricks. A God, in short, who did not really care.

The point was, what was the point?

Chapter 21

Hugo attended early morning Mass, partly to absolve himself for what he had done to Rachel, and partly to celebrate. Suddenly there was so much to celebrate. The chances were high now that he would get the job in television; Hugo a household name, a figure of remote glamour to struggling young writers such as he himself had been! It was only natural, he thought, to have discovered vanity in himself at such a prospect.

Then there was Antonia. Somewhere in the back of his mind, his mother's words still sounded the tiniest note of warning; was there really enough for a lifetime there? But Antonia was so full of joy and enthusiasm that he too was quite swept away. He thought, people who are a little short on vitality need another person to sip it from, like a tonic. Now he felt good too. And thinking about marriage, there was so much to look forward to. Aunt Mim's house was charming, with its pretty rooms and its little paved garden full of old roses and clematis. It would be so nice to live there; it would almost make up for losing the flat. Antonia had said, "Of course, you're the one with taste, darling. I shall leave all that to you. But I think the dear old thing threw in a few sticks of furniture and stuff as well; there's quite a sweet little chiffonier, and a few bits of — what's that nice flowery china called?" The wedding itself could be great fun too. Antonia's mother and he would try to swallow their mutual mistrust, and then she might let them held the reception in the grounds — a summer wedding it would have to be, of course, with Antonia in antique lace and carrying a bouquet of *gloire de Dijon* roses. Mother might be persuaded to abandon the poncho (if the paperback advance came in time, perhaps he could send her to

Jaeger with a cheque), and after the wedding everything would be fine too. One day there might be children. He could almost see them now: two little boys with fair curly hair, dressed in navy coats with velvet collars. He would hold their hands and take them to the Zoo and the Science Museum. Above all, he would be safe with Antonia. No more sudden lurches of the flesh, no more mornings of dreadful remorse. No more days lost wandering round Harrods; his time would be mapped out and accounted for.

There might also be no more mysteries. But maybe the mysteries had never been worth it anyway. Maybe that was what growing up was about.

The bell tinkled. "Lord, I am not worthy," he whispered with the priest, meaning it, of course, yet at the same time aware that God was being very good to him.

Rachel . . . the thought of her was still enough to send a shiver through him. Yes, he had behaved badly, there was no doubt about that. Yet as the Mass came to its climax, he wondered whether perhaps in the end, the experience might not be an altogether unhappy one for her to remember. After all, it was better that her first seduction had been at the hands of someone like himself rather than some spotty youth fumbling in the back of his father's car. Did that make it better? Well, perhaps not quite, and yet . . .

The bell rang again. "Say but the word, Lord, and my soul shall be healed." He buried his head in his hands, and awaited the miracle.

"Flu," said Sister Mark scornfully, "people like Sister Schol don't get flu."

But Sister Louis and Reverend Mother had decided that for the moment this was what they were going to call it. Morale was so low that Reverend Mother did not want it to sink any lower. "Well, she has now," said Sister Louis firmly.

"In that case why don't I take her up a cup of tea? Just to show a bit of charity?"

"No", said Sister Louis. "I don't think that would be a good idea at all."

The huge box of chocolates (a present from a lady in Crouch End who had found a lost cat with a prayer to the Virgin) lay on the coffee table before Anne Marie. Steven and Dermot and the rest of them were in the kitchen having a fight over something or the other. Anne Marie considered the chocolates. Should she have the orange cream or the strawberry whirl? She waved her plump little finger over the box for a while and then began to dip.

> Not because you're dirty
> Not because you're clean,
> Not because your mother
> Says you're the fairy queen

Her finger landed on the orange cream. She picked it up and ate it. It was yummy. She thought a moment and then ate the strawberry whirl as well.

Silence. It was what she had taken the veil to find, that elected silence that protected and held you. It was the stillness that led to the heart of the mystery.

But the silence was not always silent, the stillness was not always still, that was what she had discovered these last few days since . . . what? Her memory was so bad.

She was not ill, of course. She was only in this bed because her legs wouldn't carry her. They wanted her to eat, but couldn't they see it didn't matter any more? She didn't need food. God would nourish her as he had nourished Saint Catherine, on no food but the communion wafer.

It was dark now. All the other nuns were asleep. She didn't sleep any more either. There was too much to listen for, the heavenly singing, the clamouring voices. If only they would slow down just a little so that she could hear them.

What happened the other day? She tried to remember. Sometimes it came close, then it went again. She had been very unhappy, she remembered that, she had wept and shouted, but all that was over now. She didn't want to weep any more.

How nice it was here in the infirmary. How empty and silent, moonlight streaming through the high windows on to bare white beds. From time to time she heard the tremulous chimes of the clock. Twelve, one, two. The dense and dead middle of the night. A city where millions upon millions lay in their beds and slept. Slept away the wonders, slept away the voices. . . . Whose? Saint Catherine, was it yours? Saint Teresa, pierced by love, was it yours?

She watched as the door of the infirmary slowly opened. At once, brighter than moonlight there was a beam of intense clear light. A child stood there, a young child in a white gown, barelegged with short soft light hair. For a moment he stood there smiling gently, and then held out a hand to her. "Come," he said softly, "Come."

She pushed back the blankets and swung her legs out of the bed. Though they had refused to carry her the other day now they moved to her will. The child smiled, encouragingly.

"Where shall I go?" she said.

"To the chapel. There is someone there to see you."

She followed him through the sleeping convent. Though it was dark in the corridor a silvery trail marked his footsteps, reflecting in the glittering parquet and splashing the walls with light. She could see as clearly as if it were day. Along corridors they went and down stairs. There were flowers outside the chapel, a great mound of yellow roses. At the chapel door, the child stopped and turned to her, still smiling. Slowly the door swung open, and there was a great light.

She went in and the door swung silently behind her. The marble floor was cool on her bare feet and the scent of roses was in her nostrils. The light glowed and glowed, expanding like the opening petals of a flower and then she heard a soft voice. "Clare," said the voice, "Clare," using the name that no one had used for years, and no one then so lovingly. She looked up into the heart of the light as it moved and shifted and settled to reveal

Her standing there at the heart of it all smiling, a veil over Her beautiful hair, white dress purer than lilies, face more beautiful than the sun, holding out Her arms, smiling. . . .

And at last, there it was, sweeping over her, that overwhelming joy, that perfect happiness towards which she had striven and toiled all her years in the convent. Now she knew what it felt like, and standing before the figure that shone for her in front of the altar, she smiled back and gave herself up to the flood. . . .

"If he wants to mess around with her, fine," said the girl behind Rachel. "But I'm not going to be there waiting for him when he decides to come back, that's all. I'll tell him so, too."

"You don't want to be so *available*," said her friend. "Let him stew. Don't keep ringing him up all the time."

"I can ring him up if I want to. *She* does. Why can't I?"

"Yes, but you'll make him think you're *chasing* him, you moron. Just play it cool. Hey, Rachel, what's the question for that English homework tonight?"

"'How far does the tragedy of Othello arise from his own character and how far from Fate and the machinations of others,'" said Rachel without turning round.

"God, how *boring*. I think Shakespeare is so *boring*."

"Rachel doesn't think so. She think's he's marvellous, don't you."

"Who's marvellous?"

"Shakespeare, you idiot."

"No, I don't," said Rachel.

"Hey, Rachel, there's this Dulwich boy's party tonight. Some of us are going to gatecrash. Want to come?"

"No," said Rachel. She began to walk faster.

The other two girls grinned and exchanged glances and then forgot her. "God, these bloody first years! Why do they have to *push*? Just you look out, Tessa White!"

At the door a press of girls had gathered. Rachel, caught in the crowd, sighed and clutched her bag. Plump Sister Monica was on duty by the door fussing like a mother hen. "Now then, Sarah

Mason, chin up. Don't slouch or they'll take you for a silly comprehensive girl."

"Which we will be soon, won't we, Sister?" said Sarah Mason cheekily.

"Now, you be quiet," said Sister. "Laura Webber — don't tell me you're going out like that. Just you go back to the cloakroom and tidy yourself up. You too, Camilla. Look at your scarf. Come along, Linda. Emma. Kate. Come *along*. Rachel, hello, dear. Goodness what a face. Cheer up. God likes happy faces, you know, not long gloomy ones. Claudia dear, don't *push*."

Rachel caught her breath. There was no God; there never had been. Nothing held up the canopy of the sky, no hand caught the falling sparrow. She stumbled out into a world in which she was quite alone.